W
Sco

THE DESERT RIDER

The Desert Rider had acquired a considerable reputation as a nemesis for lawbreakers in the Southwest; few knew that the legendary character was really a Texas Ranger, who found it practical to conceal his identity. If they'd known, the double-crossing railroad men with whom Vane was dealing might have been less frisky.

Two railroads, the M&K and the C&P were building through the Chamisal Hills. Pride as well as fortunes was at stake, and Matt Clemon of the M&K was determined that nothing should keep his line from winning out. So he sent one of his men to pose as a cattleman, figuring he could then throw a monkey wrench into the C&P without suspicion being cast on the Big Boss. However, little threads that would have meant nothing to the average man were tied together by Vane into a tight noose.

THE DESERT RIDER

Leslie Scott

GUNSMOKE

This hardback edition 2008
by BBC Audiobooks Ltd
by arrangement with
Golden West Literary Agency

ISBN 978 1 405 68181 0

British Library Cataloguing in Publication Data available.

Printed and bound in Great Britain by
Antony Rowe Ltd., Chippenham, Wiltshire

Leslie Scott was born in Lewisburg, West Virginia. During the Great War, he joined the French Foreign Legion and spent four years in the trenches. In the 1920s he worked as a mining engineer and bridge builder in the western American states and in China before settling in New York. A bar-room discussion in 1934 with Leo Margulies, who was managing editor for Standard Magazines, prompted Scott to try writing fiction. He went on to create two of the most notable series characters in Western pulp magazines. In 1936, Standard Magazines launched, and in *Texas Rangers*, Scott under the house name of **Jackson Cole** created Jim Hatfield, Texas Ranger, a character whose popularity was so great with readers that this magazine featuring his adventures lasted until 1958. When others eventually began contributing Jim Hatfield stories, Scott created another Texas Ranger hero, Walt Slade, better known as *El Halcon*, the Hawk, whose exploits were regularly featured in *Thrilling Western*. In the 1950s Scott moved quickly into writing book-length adventures about both Jim Hatfield and Walt Slade in long series of original paperback Westerns. At the same time, however, Scott was also doing some of his best work in hardcover Westerns published by Arcadia House; thoughtful, well-constructed stories, with engaging characters and authentic settings and situations. Among the best of these, surely, are *Silver City* (1953), *Longhorn Empire* (1954), *The Trail Builders* (1956), and *Blood on the Rio Grande* (1959). In these hardcover Westerns, many of which have never been reprinted, Scott proved himself highly capable of writing traditional Western stories with characters who have sufficient depth to change in the course of the narrative and with a degree of authenticity and historical accuracy absent from many of his series stories.

THE DESERT RIDER

CHAPTER I

Captain Jim McNelty, commander of the Frontier Battalion of the Texas Rangers, bent his shaggy brows over the letter. From time to time he muttered under his mustache. It was plain that Captain Jim was not in a good temper. Suddenly he raised his head and shot a glance at the tall young man lounging comfortably in a chair on the far side of his desk.

"Tom," he said, "know anything about railroad building?"

"A little," Tom Vane admitted.

"You should," grunted Captain Jim. "Had a couple of years in engineering college before your dad got killed, didn't you?"

"Three," Vane corrected. "Did considerable field work during summer vacations, including some railroading, if that's what you're getting at."

"Never worked at engineering otherwise, though,"

Captain Jim stated, rather than asked.

Vane's steady gray-green eyes, that usually seemed to hold laughter in their depths, crinkled a little at the corners.

"Guess you have the answer to that one, sir," he replied. "And guess you know the reason."

"Uh-huh, guess I do," Captain Jim nodded. "And I guess I'm the 'reason' why you never followed it up. Recollect when I hauled you into my office for a little talk. That was right after rustlers shot your dad and ran off his cows. You were all set to track 'em down and gun 'em. I was in favor of that, all right, but I had to show you that riding the vengeance trail on your own is a mighty risky business and liable to end you up on the wrong side of the law. That's why I offered you a job with the Rangers, so you could do the chore in the right way. Well, you did it, and did it right. Remember I told you it would be okay with me if you left the outfit as soon as you finished the chore."

Tom Vane, whose eyes had turned coldly gray at the mention of the murder of his father, smiled, the corners of his rather wide mouth quirking upward.

"I remember," he said. "But I suspect that you had a good notion that once I was in I would stay in. Took quite a while to bring Dad's killers to justice, and by that time I was a Ranger. I've never regretted it. As to the engineering angle, I haven't dropped that. I've kept up my studies, and, as you'll recall, my knowledge of engineering has come in handy more than once in the course of Ranger work. I'm young and have plenty of time, if I get all that's coming to me. If I don't, it won't matter anyhow. I figure to end up an engineer, but I aim to stick with the Rangers for a while yet. Darn it, I like my job!"

The captain nodded. "You've made considerable of a reputation as a Ranger during the past few years," he commented. "Especially with Burks over in the Nueces country and with Arrington up in the Panhandle. It was up there folks started calling you the Desert Rider, I believe."

"That's right," Vane agreed. "When I had the chore of running down the Amarillo Raiders. I was convinced their hole-up was somewhere in the Tucumcari Desert. I spent weeks riding over that burned-out section before I found it, in that mess of cliffs and dunes the Indians in the old days called the Yellow Houses. Folks up there didn't know I was a Ranger, and I guess my continual prowling around the wastelands occasioned comment and conjecture. Anyhow, somebody tacked that fool name onto me, and it stuck."

"And now the Desert Rider is considerable of a legend throughout the Southwest," the captain remarked. "Well, I'm glad to have you back with me, and I've got a little chore lined up for you that may be a mite hefty for even the Desert Rider. But you seem to be at your best at undercover work and I've decided to give you a whirl at it. Here's a letter from old Jim Dunn, General Manager of the C & P Railroad. Believe you know him?"

"Yes," Vane nodded, "I worked on several cases in which 'Jaggers' Dunn, as they call him, was interested. A fine man. We got quite friendly."

"Yep, he's considerable of a character," nodded the captain. "Took over the C & P when it was just a couple of streaks of rust that didn't pay expenses. He built it into a great trunkline and he's continually expanding. Read the letter."

Vane took the letter, and read:

Dear Jim:

Things are in something of a mixup over here. As you doubtless know, I'm in a hot railroad building race. The C & P, my road, and the M & K, of which Matthew Clemon is president, are building west, with the Pass our first objective and later on the Pacific. There are valuable mail and express contracts at stake, as well as millions of dollars worth of shipping business. Naturally, the rivalry is rather strong. If that were all, I wouldn't give it much thought. I'm used to such things. But considerable personal conflict has developed, and it is trickling down through the general personnel, with bad results.

We've had a good deal of trouble—shootings, knifings, fights, destruction of property. Nobody killed so far, but the situation bids fair to get out of hand with more serious results likely. Sheriff Boone Hilton of the county over which we are building at present is a good man, but I'm afraid the situation is more than he can cope with. Besides, he has considerable trouble of another nature on his hands. Widespread rustling of late, and other depredations. So if you can spare a few Rangers and have them stationed here, it would go far toward preserving law and order and would undoubtedly prevent more serious trouble.

Such was the gist of the letter. Vane handed it back to the captain without comment, and waited.

"Dunn ain't given to exaggeration, and if he says things are bad, they're liable to be worse," said Captain Jim. "I know something about the M & K set-up. There are some hard men at the head of that outfit. Their respect for the law goes just far enough to enable them usually to keep in the clear of it. And their knowledge of the law is only surpassed by their knowledge of how it can be evaded. When Dunn says he needs Rangers, he needs 'em all right. The catch of it is I haven't any troop of Rangers to spare right now. Familiar with the Chamizal Hills country over to the west, Tom?"

"Vaguely," Vane replied. "I know the country to the south and west of there quite well."

Captain Jim nodded. "Reckon that's good enough, but I'll give you a few pointers," he said. "Roma is the country seat. The C & P is passing through Roma. Farther north is the M & K line. Their railheads at present are a bit west of Roma, driving through the Chamizal Hills. The C & P has a big construction camp east and north of Roma, and I understand they're building it into a permanent town, with yards and shops, to relieve the pressure on Sanders, their division point twenty miles east of Roma. Get the layout?"

"Yes," Vane answered. "Looks to me like Roma is likely the focal point of the trouble."

"So I'd say," agreed the captain. "It's cow country headquarters, and some of the big owners are sort of on the prod against the railroads. They don't want 'em hornin' in on their preserves and bringing in new folks and new customs. One in particular I know of, an old shorthorn by the name of Clate Bradshaw who owns the best spread west of the Pecos. He's run the section right up to the hilt for a good many years. He's plumb sot against the railroads and I'd say is the spearpoint of the opposition. Which is something to keep in mind, seeing as Dunn complains that obstacles are being thrown in his way. That sheriff Dunn mentions is okay, but I've a notion he was sort of behind the door when they were passing out brains. He'll back any play you make, but you'll have to do the thinking. Now I'd say the best thing for you to do is take a freight train to Sanders. It will save you a hundred-mile ride and get you there quicker. I'll arrange to have your horse corralled in a stock car so you'll have him ready to hand when you hit Sanders. Okay son, good ridin'!"

Three hours later, Tom Vane superintended the loading of Smoke, his big blue Moros, into a stock car in which a stall had been hastily built. Then he retired to the caboose to share the quarters of the conductor and the rear brakeman. He drowsed comfortably most of the long trip.

"Yes, one more stop for water before we reach Sanders," the conductor answered his question as the sun climbed over the edge of the world to bring a golden morning to the rangeland. "Yes, you'll have time to look in on your horse."

As soon as the long train jolted to a stop, with the panting engine alongside the huge red watertank,

Vane dropped from the caboose steps and walked swiftly to the head end. He found Smoke okay and walked on to the engine.

The old engineer leaned out his window. "What say, cowboy; like to ride in the cab for a spell?" he asked, with a friendly grin.

Vane smiled back at the engineer. His gaze travelled over the big locomotive hissing and purring while water gushed into the tender-tank from the overhead pipe the sooty fireman held in place over the manhole. He glanced back toward the distant caboose.

"Not a bad notion," he accepted the invitation. "Save me from walking back or swinging onto the caboose as she comes by."

"Always better to walk back and take her standin'," cautioned the engineer. "Grabbin' a crummy on the fly is a job for a trained railroader. It ain't the same as a horse, feller."

"Nope, not exactly," Vane agreed gravely as he swung up the steps of the engine cab. "You always know where the caboose will be when you reach for it. Can't tell about a horse. He may take a notion to head in another direction."

The engineer glanced suspiciously at Vane's sober countenance. He had a feeling he was being joshed by this big broad-shouldered, deep-chested young fellow with a grin quirking at the corners of his mouth. He chuckled as Vane's sunny eyes met his.

"Maybe you got somethin' there son," he conceded. "Well, ridin' a spell in the cab will sort of bust up the monotony. And you can help keep an eye out on the track ahead while that fat tallowpot is shovellin' coal into this hog. Got to keep a close watch nowadays, with them blasted M & K rascals and the ranchers out to make trouble.

"Day before yesterday they greased the rails on Chiso Hill, back to the east of here, and had rocks and cross-ties piled on the track at the bottom of the hill. Work train slid down them greased rails despite everything the hogger could do to step her. Banged into that mess on the track and derailed the engine and four cars. Nobody hurt, but just dumb luck they wasn't. That sort of thing's gettin' to be regular of late. And from here to Sanders, and on towards Roma —that's close to as far as the steel's laid in the buildin'—is the real trouble section. We're close to the line the M & K's racin' us to the Pass with, and the race's neck-and-neck, and they're doin' everything they can to slow us up."

"Having real trouble, then?" Vane commented.

"You're darn right," grunted the engineer. He twisted his neck around to glance up at the fireman.

"All right, you lucky work dodger," he called.

"You've rested long enough. She's runnin' over already. Hop down here and get busy."

The fireman swore cheerfully at him, banged the manhole cover shut and came sliding down the coal to the deck. He grinned at Vane, opened the furnace door and glanced at his fire.

"Okay," he told the hoghead. "Stop gabbin' for a minute and let's go. And try and get up a little speed today. You ain't drivin' a freight wagon any more, like you used to. Wheels was put on this 'gine to turn over. Try and turn 'em a little today. It'll be noon 'fore we get to Sanders, anyhow, and I'm hungry."

"You're always hungry," snorted the aggrieved hogger. "I don't see how a feller with only one mouth can eat so much. All right, let's go, and I could use a little steam on this run. I figure I'm the only engineer in the country who can pull a train without steam. Had to learn how since you been shovelin' coal, or pretendin' to shovel it for me."

The fireman winked at Vane and hopped onto his seatbox. Vane lounged comfortably in the gangway, leaning against the rounded corner of the tender, which was pleasantly cool to his back, and gazing ahead along the twin lengths of steel rails shimmering in the Texas sunshine. On and on they stretched, until the parallel lines seemed to meet, climbing a heavy grade to the crest of a distant rise. Thick chaparral encroached on the right-of-way with bristles of trees farther back.

The engineer blew three long blasts to call in the flagman. He leaned out the cab window, looking back. Finally he got a highball from the conductor, settled himself comfortably on his seatbox and crackled the throttle, kicking open the cylinder cocks at the same moment. Steam hissed out on either side. The stack boomed wetly. The great drivers turned over, grinding on the sand that ran in a thin stream from the pipes under the wheels. The drivers slipped. The stack thundered, shooting up a cloud of black smoke.

"That's right," growled the fireman. "Tear my fire to pieces. Will you ever learn to start a train without makin' the engine do a square dance?"

The engineer twisted the sand blower valves a little wider. He opened the throttle again. The stack boomed. The drivers ground against the high iron. Back along the train couplers clanked and jangled as the big engine took up the slack. The drivers turned steadily. The stack began its rhythmic song. The long line of cars rolled ahead. The engineer hooked the reverse lever a little higher on the quadrant, opened the throttle a little more. The train picked up speed; cars began to rock and sway. The fireman hopped down and bailed coal into the firebox. He clanged the door shut and hopped back onto the seatbox. Vane glanced at the growth flickering by, turned his attention to the track ahead.

Louder and louder thundered the stack as the engine breasted the grade. The engineer dropped the reverse lever down the quadrant a few notches, widened the throttle. Soon the speed slowed as the locomotive pounded up the grade with the whole train tugging hard on the drawbar. The fireman was working almost continually now. Both injectors were wide open, pouring streams of water into the quivering boiler. The steam gauge hand rose slowly and steadily till it touched the two hundred pounds pressure point. There it hung, quivering. A feathery squirrel-tail of steam drifted back from the safety valve.

"There aint a better fireman on the division," the old hogger observed in low tones to Vane. "Look at the way he's holdin' the steam. Smack up against the peg. And we need every pound on this grade. He'll get a chance to rest a bit once we get over the hump. Five miles of downgrade, where I just let 'em roll."

Up and up, with the exhaust booming, the side-rods clanking, the crash of steel on steel blending in a vibrating roar. The gleaming ribbons rolled steadily behind. The growth marched steadily forward, flickered beside the cab windows and drifted to the rear.

The crest of the rise loomed against the sky and flattened slowly as the laboring locomotive closed the distance. And on and on stretched the web of ties and rails that the Apaches named the Thunder Trail.

"Say cowboy," said the engineer, "climb up the coal gate chains, will you, and see if you can spot that darned head brakeman. He should be over here in the cab by now, helpin' to keep a watch ahead. Don't know what's holdin' him up. Haven't seen him since we stopped for water. In the crummy, poundin' his ear, chances are. Don't see why the con don't rout him out and send him up here where he belongs."

Vane nodded and clambered up the chains till he could look across the tops of the swaying box-cars.

"Don't see him," he called to the hoghead.

The engineer swore peevishly. "Good for nothin' loafer," he grumbled. "And we need everybody on the job today. We got fifteen carloads of dynamite in this string. Enough to blow Texas clean to Mexico. Well, here we go over the top."

Vane eased down the chains, still standing in the indenture formed by the rounded corners of the tank. The locomotive was just nosing over the brush-crowned crest of the rise. On either side the growth was almost close enough to touch.

The engineer speculated Vane's broad back. "Golly, but he's a big feller," he mused. "Way over six feet tall, Nice too, but I'll bet he's one tough hombre if somethin' stirs him up. The way he wears them two big guns says business! Wonder who he is, anyhow? 'Pears to pack considerable drag along the line. The con told me that stock car for his horse we picked up back at Rio was hooked on by order of the general superintendent himself."

The locomotive topped the rise and lurched down the far sag, the throttle wide open, the reverse lever "down in the corner," the exhaust pounding a slow thunder. The cars begain humping over the crest, moving at a crawl. Vane stepped down from the last chain, still partially shielded by the jutting corner of the tender.

From the growth on either side roared a blaze of gunfire. The fireman toppled from his seat and thudded to the deck, to lie without sound or motion. The engineer floundered sideways with a scream of pain, fell beside the dead fireman, writhing and moaning, blood widening a dark stain on the front of his shirt.

From the growth poured half a dozen men, yelping with triumph. They rushed for the cab steps of the slowly moving locomotive, guns smoking.

But the Desert Rider was not a man to be shot at with impunity. His bronzed hands flashed down and up. Both his big guns spouted flame and smoke.

Yells of pain and consternation echoed the boom of the reports. Two men went down, thrashing and wallowing in the brush. A third reeled, lurched around and staggered for cover. The remaining three also dived for the brush, shooting as they ran.

Vane fired again. Another howl showed he had scored a hit. Then a gun cracked from the brush. The Desert Rider lurched back, sagged against the chains and slid slowly to the deck to lie motionless beside the dead fireman and the moaning engineer. The great locomotive, bereft of a guiding hand, thundered down the grade, gaining speed with every turn of its ponderous drivers. Behind it the long train lurched and swayed as more and more of the length hit the downgrade. The dynamite cars pounded over the crest, their red warning posters glaring in the sunlight.

CHAPTER II

It was the old engineer's pawing hands and yammering voice that roused Vane from the fog of red flashes and clammy blackness that coiled about his brain. Mechanically he raised his bloody face from the deck and glared around with eyes that for the moment but dimly took in details. He shook his head, raised trembling fingers to the slight gash just above his left temple.

"Creased," he muttered. "Must have knocked me cold." He shook his head again, trying to free his mind of cobwebs. The chattering speech of the engineer began to take on definite meaning.

"What's the matter, old timer?" he mumbled.

The engineer's voice rose in a thin wail, urgent, compelling. Vane abruptly understood what he was saying.

"You've got to stop her, cowboy!" yammered the

voice. "You've got to stop her. She'll leave the iron on the curve at Sanders. She'll blow the town off the map. Fifteen cars of dynamite!"

"Stop what?" Vane wondered dully. Then suddenly he realized where he was. Realized, too, that the locomotive cab was rocking and jumping like a steamer in a heavy sea. He scrambled to his hands and knees, weaving and lurching.

"Do what I tell you!" panted the wounded engineer. "Get up there—close the throttle—push it all the way down toward the boilerhead. Then put on the air—the short lever stickin' out there. Not all at once—easy—easy."

Vane's faculties returned with a rush. He bounded to his feet, clutching at the coal gate chains for support. For a moment he stool weaving; then he reeled across the swaying deck and onto the seatbox.

"Do just as I say—" began the engineer in agonized gasps.

"Quiet!" Vane told him as he slammed the throttle shut. "I know what to do. Don't try to talk. You'll choke to death on blood. Try to hold yourself steady. I'm using the air."

Slowly he opened the valve, notching the lever around carefully. He heard the shoes grind against the tires. He eased off a little, then applied the air again, harder this time. The grind became a screech.

The locomotive bucked like a living thing. Then the long string of loaded cars jammed their million pounds hard against the drawbar. The engine shot forward on screaming wheels. Vane opened the valve wide, taking a chance on derailment. Tensely he watched the needle drop down the gauge as the pressure in the reservoirs fell. The train had not, so far as he could tell, slackened speed in the least. He threw the valve back to port, releasing the brakes. Closed it. The air pressure swiftly built up as the pumps clanked and hammered. Again he threw the lever, all the way around this time, into the "big hole." The howl of tortured metal rose above the thundering roar of the runaway. It seemed to Vane the speed slackened a little. Leaning out the window, he gazed down the long slope. Far below, huddled in its canyon mouth, the buildings looking like doll houses in the distance, was the town of Sanders, the railroad line sweeping around it in a rather sharp curve.

Vane shook his head, released the air. Slowly the pressure built up again. Too slowly. He glanced at the steam gauge. The needle was falling.

Muttering an oath, he slipped to the deck, stepping over the engineer who had sunk into a stupor. He was forced to move the body of the dead fireman. He flung open the fire door, twirling the blower wide at the same time. The clang of the shovel echoed through the rocking cab. Black smoke boiled from the stack. Vane swung the door shut and climbed back onto the seatbox. He glanced around.

Already the town was appreciably nearer. He perked the whistle wide open and tied down the cord. The eerie wail added to the general uproar.

Again he applied the air. The rocketing train slowed a little more. But not enough. To hit the curve at the present speed would mean disaster. Setting his teeth, he did what any experienced railroader shrinks from doing under such circumstances; the last resort. He hurled the reverse bar back to the last notch in the quadrant and opened the throttle.

The former uproar was nothing to what now took place. The locomotive leaped and bucked. The great drivers, spinning and slipping in reverse, planed curling steel shavings from the rails. The crash of pounding drawbars flung back from the encroaching growth. Clots of fire streaked through the smoke and steam bellowing from the stack. Vane was nearly hurled from the seatbox.

The crowding cars nudged the engine, sending it shrieking along on sliding wheels. The safety valve opened with a roar. The straining boiler groaned and creaked.

Howling, thundering, crashing, the runaway tore

down the grade toward the town in the canyon mouth. Vane could see men pouring from the shops and other buildings, staring up the grade, then turning to flee the destruction hurtling toward them. He slammed the throttle shut, hurled the reverse lever forward. The engine shot ahead. Again he reversed full over. Again the crash of jammed couplers, the howling of the tortured tires.

"That did it!" he muttered. "She's slowing, and we're still on the iron. He dropped the reverse bar into forward motion again and applied every ounce of air. As the pressure screeched through the port and the reservoir hand dropped, the long train slowed to a decent speed. She was under control. Vane exhaled the breath he had unconsciously been holding. He settled back on the seatbox, jockeying the engine brake as the drawbars bumped and grumbled. Again he swept the automatic brake valve lever around the drum. Again the release. Then, as the pressure built up, a steady application.

The engine careened as it struck the curve, rounded it on grinding wheels. Squarely in front of the station the long train came to a stop.

CHAPTER III

Men were running up from every direction. Vane gathered the unconscious engineer in his arms and slid down the cab steps. Instantly he was surrounded by a jostling throng bellowing questions.

"Quiet!" he thundered in a voice that stilled the turmoil. "This feller is bad hurt. Where can I find a doctor?"

A huge man with hard blue eyes and a tight mouth came shouldering through the crowd that opened respectfully upon recognizing him.

"I'm Barrington, the division superintendent," he told Vane. "Follow me. We've got a sort of hospital operating over at the edge of the yards. Old Ben Worthington, isn't it? Bring him along cowboy; you can tell me about it later."

The superintendent was evidently a man of few words. He did not speak again until they reached the makeshift hospital at the edge of the yards. Then his roaring voice got instant attention.

A capable-looking doctor took charge of the engineer. "Think we can pull him through," he said, after a swift examination. "He's old, but he's tough as rawhide. The bullet went through, high up. I don't believe there is any serious internal hemorrhage, and it is not a wind wound, thank heaven. But if he hadn't been gotten here in a hurry, it would have been different."

"He got here in a hurry, all right," Barrington returned dryly. "And now, cowboy, perhaps you can tell me what happened."

Vane told him, in terse sentences. As the tale unfolded, the big super's face darkened and his eyes blazed. He shook his fist to the north and swore viciously.

"This is too much!" he said. "We've stood for plenty, but cold-blooded murder is too much."

Vane regarded him a moment, then spoke. "I've told you what happened, sir," he said. "Maybe you can tell me what this is all about. I was sort of in the middle and feel I have a right to know."

"Reckon you have," Barrington instantly conceded. "And I want to thank you for saving old Ben's life and, the chances are, quite a few others. If that dynamite had cut loose, there wouldn't be anything left of this town but a grease spot. What's back of this is bitter railroad competition, and mule-headed local opposition, that's all. We're racing the M & K to the Pass over to the west. Whoever gets there first, the M & K or the C & P, will control the trans-continental traffic through the southwest. There are valuable mail and express contracts at stake, among other things."

Vane stared at the superintendent. "You mean to tell me, sir, that a reputable corporation and respectable ranch owners would back a thing like this?" he asked incredulously.

Barrington shrugged his heavy shoulders. "Who else, then?" he countered. "I'll admit I would never have believed that Matt Clemon, the president of the M & K, or old Clate Bradshaw—he's the biggest ranch owner hereabouts—would be capable of what happened today. Clemon is a hard man and not too scrupulous. He's good at short cuts and shrewd practices that, while they may be legal, are certainly not ethical. He's made us plenty of trouble. Of course he has considerable at stake. If we get to the Pass first and build through it, he will have to use our tracks from Sierra Blanca on through the Pass. Whoever controls the Pass holds the whip hand. Controlling the southern route as we do, we have the advantage for the moment. Old Man Dunn, the General Mana-

ger of the C & P, saw this thing building up quite
a few years ago. He made it his business to get control of the southern route long before the M & K
actually contemplated extending their holdings to
such an extent as to make them a system reaching
the west coast. When Clemon, the president and controlling stockholder of the M & K, began acquiring
his right-of-way, he was almighty surprised to find
that Jaggers Dunn had gotten ahead of him. He
rared and charged, but he couldn't do anything about
it. At least nothing legitimate. He got busy and acquired the northern route, which runs around the
head of Sanders Canyon. He's been building mighty
fast, but hasn't been able to quite catch up with us,
although at present he's mighty close."

"But," Vane pointed out, "even if the M & K did
lose the race to the Pass, they'd still prosper, passing
over the fine cattle and farming lands to the north.
That is, if the C & P will lease them trackage through
the Pass."

"That's right," agreed Barrington, "and they don't
have to worry about getting a lease. Dunn is a square-
shooter from the word go and he never plays a dog-
in-the-manger role. He'll let 'em through. But the
southern route controls the cream of the business.
And you can count on it, if the M & K gets there
first, we'll not use their tracks through the Pass. We'll

be stuck with a short line with its terminus at Sierra Blanca. Also, if that happens, Mr. Dunn's other plans will fall through. He aims to build a line southwest of here to Mexico. That will tap the mining, cattle and other trades from Mexico and the whole southwest. It will mean such a boom for the section as has never been seen. All the transportation they now have is by way of cart trains and freight wagon lines. That holds that section down. If we can just run our line down there, they'll know real prosperity. But we can't do it without our line to the Pacific. The M & K knows that, and they're doing everything they can to hold us up."

Vane nodded thoughfully. Barrington's argument was plausible, but if he was right, it meant such a railroad war as the southwest had never seen.

"What about the rancher you mentioned?" he asked.

Barrington seemed to hesitate. "Clate Bradshaw, owner of the Cross C, has caused us plenty of trouble," he said slowly. "As I said, his holding is the biggest and best in the section. He's the most influential man in this end of the state. Our western line passes across his land, and so will the proposed one to the southwest. Bradshaw fought us tooth and nail, and is still fighting. He opposed Jaggers Dunn when he was trying for the franchise in the legislature. Dunn beat him, the statute of Eminent Domain was invoked and we got our right-of-way; but Bradshaw didn't stop fighting. He's smart enough to realize that the building of the southwest line depends on our getting through the Pass before the M & K, and is concentrating on slowing us up in every way he can. He hasn't any use for the M & K either, but he's willing to use the M & K as a club to beat our brains out. If he whips us, he'll be able to hand the M & K a few licks, or thinks he will be."

"The M & K right-of-way doesn't pass over his holdings, then?"

"No," replied Barrington. "Their line, in this section, passes across the Rocking H, which is owned by a fellow named Wesley Hardin, a comparative newcomer to the section. Hardin didn't like the notion, either, but I guess he figured he couldn't hold up progress. So he took his price for his land and let it go at that. He's a friend of Bradshaw's though, and I think Bradshaw can rely on Hardin to lend a hand to further his schemes."

"But why should Bradshaw object to the railroad coming through?" Vane asked. "It would just mean more prosperity for him."

"Bradshaw doesn't need prosperity," Barrington replied. "'He's rich. He's an old-time cattle baron with more money than he knows what to do with.

He says the railroad will bring in farmers and others. He calls 'em nesters. He's right about that. He doesn't want the prevailing order changed. He doesn't want folks he can't dictate to, as he does to the other ranchers and most of the mine owners. He's a rabidly partisan politician and has for years decided who shall hold office in the section and who shall represent it over in the capital. I figure he isn't such a bad feller personally, but he loves power and has been used to it for years. He doesn't look favorably on any change in his status, even though it will mean prosperity and advancement for the many."

The discussion was interrupted by the entrance of the conductor of the freight train.

"What in blazes happened?" he demanded, panting for breath. "They tell me Hogan is dead and old Ben dyin'? What—"

"Just a minute," Vane interrupted. "Conductor, where is your head brakeman?"

"Why," the con replied in surprised tones, "he was on the engine, wasn't he?"

"No," Vane replied quietly, "he was not. He said he was going back to look for hot boxes when we stopped for water. We thought he was in the caboose."

"He wasn't," the conductor repeated.

Vane turned to Barrington. "I've got a notion,

sir," he said, "you'd better send a search party out to look for him, or what's left of him."

"Good grief!" exclaimed the super. "You don't think—"

"I do," Vane interrupted. "Chances are that was part of the scheme—to get him out of the way so there would only be two men in the engine cab. The brush grows close to the tracks all along there, and he was walking back on the outside of the curve. Couldn't be seen from either the engine or the caboose. Yes, I'm afraid they did for him. That would make it easier for them. They didn't count on me being in the cab, of course."

"I didn't know we were runnin' away till it was too late," remarked the conductor. "Thought we were rollin' purty fast, but before I caught on that we were plumb out of control it was too late for me to do anything about it. I tried to stop 'em with the air from the caboose, but the shoes wouldn't hold."

"You caused me trouble while I was trying to build up the air pressure—fiddling with that valve back there," Vane observed.

Barrington put a stop to further talk. "Ed," he told the conductor, "go find the sheriff—he's in Sanders today; spends more time here of late than he does in Roma—and tell him to get a bunch together and ride out there and see if he can find the brakeman."

"And he may find a body or two around the crest of the rise, if the rest of the bunch didn't come back and pack 'em off," Vane added. "Tell him I'd like to ride with him, if he doesn't mind. I'll go get my horse out of that stock car. Scared he's liable to be bruised black and blue with the shaking up he got."

"Young man, I'd like to have a talk with you when you come back to town," Barrington said. "I want to thank you properly for what you did. Look me up soon as you get back."

Vane promised to do so. He left the hospital and hurried back to the train. An excited crowd was gathered at the station. It made way for him in respectful silence. When his errand was made clear, men hurried to assist with the chore of getting Smoke from the car. The big moros looked decidedly disgusted but appeared none the worse for his disturbing experience. It was plain, also, that he relished the notion of stretching his legs after the inactivity of the train trip.

Vane got the rig on Smoke. Then, while waiting for the sheriff to arrive, he grabbed a sandwich and a cup of coffee in a nearby restaurant. He had just returned to the street when a troop of horsemen came riding up. Foremost was a blocky old man with a drooping mustache, a lined, leathery face and frosty blue eyes. On his sagging vest was pinned a big nickel badge. He took Vane in from head to foot with a keen glance, and appeared pleased with what he saw.

"I'm Boone Hilton," he announced, reining in beside Smoke. "So you're the feller who stopped the train? Come along. Be glad to have you, and you'll know just where you left those hellions."

Vane supplied his name and shook hands with the sheriff.

"We'll have to hit the Comanche Trail over to the east of town and circle around by the north fork to get to the top of that sag," said the sheriff as the posse got under way. "The Comanche parallels the railroad to the east of the ridge. Come on; we got considerable of a ride ahead of us."

It was but five miles to the crest of the ridge by way of the railroad, but on horseback it was quite a bit farther. The posse first headed due south to skirt the hills and the broken ground. Then the direction was changed to the east, following a track that climbed ridges and dipped down sags.

Soon after the posse departed, a lone horseman rode slowly out of Sanders, headed west. Once he was well clear of the town, however, he quickened his horse's pace and sped south by west at racing speed, from time to time glancing back over his shoulder.

CHAPTER IV

"This is the trail the smugglers used, and still use at times," the sheriff remarked to Vane as they rode east at a good pace. "It runs from the lower Big Bend country and joins with the Comanche which comes straight up from the south, climbs that bunch of hills ahead and turn east. One fork, just south of the ridge we're headin' for, runs due north and crosses the M & K right-of-way."

"And that's where them hellions will have headed for, what was left of 'em," remarked a posseman. The sheriff neither contradicted nor affirmed the statement.

Another mile of fast riding and the trail dipped into a gloomy, narrow canyon thickly grown with brush. Here it wormed its way like a discouraged snake between the sloping sides, swerving around chimney rocks and huge boulders and boring through bristles of thickets.

"That's the Devil's Kitchen over there," remarked the sheriff, gesturing with his thumb toward a cluster of grotesque spires straggling along the course of the trail. "The Apaches bushwacked a whole troop of emigrants from there once. Did for all of 'em and burned their wagons. See how blacked up some of the rocks are. The oilers and not a few Texans say that smoke blackenin' was caused by the Devil cookin' a meal of bodies. But it was really caused by the burnin' wagons."

"A natural for a drygulching, all right," Vane agreed soberly. "Commands the trail going and coming." He glanced up the sloping canyon wall to the rimrock several hundred feet above. "And from up there anyone coming along this way could be seen for miles," he added.

The sheriff nodded. "This darn snake hole always gives me the creeps when I ride through it," he admitted. "Get a funny feeling along my backbone goin' past that hole-up over there. Always glad when I get past it."

The trail left the shadows of the canyon and reached the rangeland again. Another mile and it joined with the broad Comanche. Soon afterward a fork turned from the main Comanche and slanted up the side of the ridge. Twenty minutes of climbing the ridge, and directly ahead, less than a mile distant, were the twin ribbons of the railroad, shimmering in the afternoon sunshine.

As they approached the rails, Vane's eyes were studying the surface of the trail. The concentration furrow deepened between his black brows, a sure sign the Desert Rider was doing some hard thinking.

They were within a hundred yards of the right-of-way when a posseman uttered an exclamation.

"There's where they left their horses," he said, pointing to where a number of hoof marks scored the soft ground between the trail and the bristle of brush on the east.

Vane touched the sheriff's bridle arm. "Pull up a minute," he suggested. "I'd like to have a look at those prints before we mess 'em up."

The sheriff nodded agreement and brought the posse to a halt. Vane dismounted and walked slowly forward, scanning the ground as he did so. He paused beside the scoring of hoofs and studied them for some minutes. He turned and beckoned the posse to come on.

"I saw only six men when they jumped the engine," he said to the sheriff. "But more than a dozen horses were halted here. And here's something of interest," he added, pointing to the ground. "Keep it in mind, Sheriff. You'll notice that one of the cayuses had a broken calk on a front shoe. Print shows plainly."

The sheriff regarded him curiously. "Them eyes of yours don't miss much, do they?" he commented. "Uh-huh, I see it, when you point it out. But I calc'late I wouldn't have noticed it otherwise. I can't see that it shows over plain. Well, we might as well leave our bronks here and shove through the brush to the ridge top. That's where it happened, I believe you said."

Vane leading the way, the posse forged ahead. A few minutes later they were scanning the ground on the ridge crest and close to the right-of-way.

Evidence of the passage of the raiders was plain enough, in the form of trampled ground and broken twigs, but of the killers themselves, dead or alive, there was no sign.

Vane did not appear particularly surprised. "Two men were down when we rolled over," he remarked. "I don't know for sure whether they were done for, but they were hard hit. The rest of the bunch came back and packed 'em off, evidently. That was to be expected, though. Bodies can sometimes be tied up with something or somebody. Yes, they got it hard. Plenty of blood splashed around, you'll notice."

The sheriff swore wrathful agreement. "Nothin'

more we can do here, then," he said. "All right, everybody—scatter along on both sides the track and try and find that poor brakeman."

"He should not be far from the water tank down at the bottom of the sag," Vane remarked. "About a mile from here, I'd say."

They walked swiftly down the slope to the water tank, then proceeded more slowly.

"Here he is," suddenly shouted a man who had forged ahead of the others.

Faces dark with anger, the posse gathered around the body of the slain brakeman. His skull had been crushed by a heavy blow, and to make doubly sure, a long knife was driven between his shoulder blades.

"The snake-blooded devils!" growled the sheriff. "Why couldn't they just have knocked him out?" He turned and shook his fist to the north.

"I'd hate to have on my conscience what those hellions up there have on theirs," he declared. "All right, two of you fellers pick him up and bring him along. We'll pack him in on the back of the spare horse we brought with us. Let's go. There's nothin' more we can do here." He brooded a moment, then announced:

"Jasper, you and Alfreds take this feller back to town. The rest of us will ride north a ways and see if we can pick up the trail of those sidewinders. I'd sure like to line sights with 'em. I'd do my arrestin' after the shootin' was over. No sense in wastin' rope."

Vane said nothing at the moment, but his eyes were coldly gray and deep with thought.

The sun was low in the western sky when they reached the point where they left the horses.

"Let's go," said the sheriff as he swung into the saddle. But Vane stopped him before he could get under way.

"Sheriff," he said quietly, "that bunch didn't go north. They went south."

"What in blazes are you talkin' about?" demanded the old peace officer. "If they didn't go north, back to that blasted railroad camp up there, where would they go?"

"I don't know," Vane admitted, "but I do know they didn't turn north when they left here."

"How do you know?" snorted the sheriff.

"Come here," Vane told him. "Remember I pointed out to you that iron with a busted calk? Well, here go the prints of that shoe, heading south, and others around it. And look close. Do you see the blood spots? I noticed them quite a ways down the trail as we rode up here. Hop down and take a look for yourself."

Incredulously, the sheriff dismounted. But as he examined the ground closely, his expression changed.

"Blast it, feller, you're right!" he ejaculated. "They did go south. Not what does this mean?"

"I believe," Vane said slowly, "that you told me the Comanche Trail heads almost due south from where it forks. South to Mexico. That may be the answer. And if you are right in suspecting the builders of the M & K, I'd say the bunch responsible for the killings was brought in to do the job, and cleared out of the country directly afterward."

"By gosh, that sounds reasonable, replied the sheriff. "Feller, if you're right, we may have a chance to catch 'em. The Rio Grande is almighty high right now, and I don't think they'd take a chance on fordin' it at night. They'd make camp somewhere, I'd say, and if they do, we'll have a show at hittin' 'em before they get across in the mornin'. Let's go!"

They rode down the slant of the sag, Vane keenly scanning the trail the while.

"Missed a bet," he told himself. "All that talk about the M & K had me concentrating on the north and I didn't pay any attention to the trail farther south. If I had, maybe we would have had a chance to down the sidewinders. Well, reckon a feller can't think of everything."

They reached the fork and rode west along the main Comanche. But where the Comanche turned south at the point of juncture with the track leading to Sanders, Vane called a halt. He dismounted and carefully examined the ground, then turned to the sheriff.

"Wrong guess," he said quietly. "They didn't turn south here. They kept to the track through the canyon, the one that leads to town."

The sheriff swore in disgusted bewilderment. He unforked and made sure Vane had made no mistake.

"Now what's the meanin' of this?" he demanded of all and sundry. "Are they headed for the Big Bend country? This track runs there, as I told you before, Vane."

"There's a chance," Vane remarked thoughtfully, "that they circled around to the west and holed up somewhere, figuring to slide into town under cover of darkness, perhaps, by twos and threes. Reckon there's considerable traffic into Sanders?"

"Plenty," the sheriff admitted. "You may have the right slant. Well let's be movin'. Blazes! I never had such a day!"

Soon they sighted the high bluffs that walled the canyon through which the trail flowed. The sun was setting and a level flood of light poured across the crests of the canyon walls. Vane studied the ragged rimrock as they drew nearer. Suddenly he leaned forward in his saddle, peering intently toward the crest of the southern slope. His keen eyes had caught a quick flash as of shifted metal reflecting the sunlight. Then he saw shadowy movement on the rimrock, movement almost instantly swallowed by the brush that crowned the crest.

"Did you see it?" he asked the sheriff. "There was a jigger sitting a horse up there on the rimrock. He's gone now. Slid down the slope into the canyon, I think."

"I didn't see him," growled the sheriff. "Now what?"

"May have just been someone riding along up there, though what anybody would be doing up there I can't understand," Vane replied. "But it might have been somebody posted up there to spot us when we came along."

"But in the name of blazes, why?" demanded the sheriff.

"I can't answer that one," Vane said, adding grimly, "but the way things have been happening today, I figure it isn't a good notion to miss any bets. Take it easy through that gulch and keep your eyes skun."

Grumbling disgustedly, the sheriff slowed down. The others eyed the gloomy canyon mouth apprehensively. The sunlight still mellowed the heights, but the depths of the gorge were already shadowy with the promise of swiftly coming night.

A mutter ran through the ranks of the posse. Even the sheriff appeared worried.

"Do you really think those hombres might be in there waitin' for us?" he asked Vane.

The Ranger shrugged his broad shoulders. "Funny things been happening hereabouts of late, I understand," he repeated. "And I still can't figure what that rider was doing up on the crest. My advice is to assume, on the face of it, that they're not, but at the same time act as though they were. Come on, and take it easy."

Undeniably reluctant, the posse moved into the shadowy mouth of the gorge. The riders' nervousness communicated itself to the horses and they stepped gingerly, ears pricked and eyes rolling.

They covered a couple of hundred yards, the horses pacing slowly. Ahead, perhaps half as far again, was the cluster of spires and chimney rocks known as the Devil's Kitchen. The gloom was deepening and the shadows gave a disquieting illusion of stealthy movement.

Suddenly Vane held up his hand. With one accord the posse jerked to a holt, peering ahead, straining their ears. All was silent save for the raucous clamor of a bluejay somewhere ahead. As they listened, the sound persisted, angry, querulous.

"Something's got that feathered feller worked up,"

Vane said in low tones. "He's sure raising the roof. Maybe only a snake nosing around close to his nest, or a coyote under the bush. But he's sure on the prod against something. Sheriff, is it possible to get around behind that clump of rocks?"

"We ought to be able to circle around through the brush," the sheriff decided, "but it'll be rough goin'."

"It'll be rougher by the trail, if somebody does happen to be holed up behind those rocks, waiting for us," Vane answered grimly. "May be a loco notion, but I'd advise we have a look-see."

The sheriff did not stop to reason why he was obeying the suggestions of this tall, level-eyed cowhand who appeared to have taken charge of things. He merely nodded and threw a leg over his saddle.

"Let one man stay here this side of the bend with the horses," Vane said. "Come on, the rest of you, and for Pete's sake be quiet. And use your eyes and ears."

Silently the posse melted into the brush, moving with the greatest care, careful to break no twig, to overturn no stone.

"There are only six of us and, if I figured right, even counting two or three knocked out in the ruckus on the ridge top, there'll still be about ten or twelve of the hellions," Vane whispered to the sheriff as they began to veer to the west. "That's not good odds to go up against. But if we can get the jump on them, it'll sort of even the score."

It was nervous work, creeping through the gloom without knowing what they were up against. Ahead loomed the chimney rocks, towering, grotestque in the shadows, seemingly imbued with malevolent life. The brush was thinning and it was still light enough for movement to be detected by a keen-eyed watcher. Flesh crawled at the thought that even now the out-law band might be lining sights with those hoping to surprise them.

Suddenly every man stiffened to stone. From directly ahead came a quick jangle of metal, like that made by bridle irons when a horse petulantly tosses its head. For crawling moment, nobody dared to move. Then, at a whispered word from the sheriff, the stealthy advance began again.

"I think I see them," Vane whispered to the sheriff. "There to the left—alongside that big rock. Steady, we've got 'em settin'."

But just as things appeared to be going nicely, disaster struck. A posseman, a cocked gun in his hand, stepped on a loose stone that rolled beneath his foot. He floundered, tripped over a projecting root. Down went the posseman, and off went the gun with a boom that seemed to fill earth and heaven with horrific sound.

Instantly yelps of alarm sounded from the shadows beneath the rocks, then a perfect storm-blast of gun-fire. Bullets hissed through the air and clipped twigs from the bushes. A posseman howled as one tore through the flesh of his upper arm.

Tom Vane raced forward, firing with both hands. A voice rang out above the uproar:

"There he is! Get him!"

Slugs screeched past the Ranger. One nicked his hand. Another ripped the sleeve of his shirt. A third turned his hat sideways on his head.

But weaving, ducking, he was an elusive target, and his own blazing guns answered the outlaws shot for shot. A wail of pain split the air. Another, and a torrent of curses. Vane sent lead hissing toward the swirling shadows beneath the rock. The possemen were also firing as fast as they could pull trigger. Back and forth through the gloom spurted the red lances of flame. The screams and stamping of frightened horses added to the uproar. The posse closed in for the kill.

Again the commanding voice rang out, clear above the pandemonium.

"Hightail! Get out of this!"

Followed a tremendous crashing in the brush, a popping of saddle leather, then the beat of fast hoofs racing down the canyon.

"After 'em!" roared Sheriff Hilton. "Get the horses!"

The posse tore back through the brush to where their mounts were supposed to be waiting, only to face fresh trouble. Smoke alone stood quietly in the trail. The man who had been left in charge of the cayuses was raving and cursing and wiping blood from his face.

"What happened?' bawled the sheriff. "Where are our bronks?"

"Gone!" the man shouted back. "Stampeded, the whole bunch of em. The shootin' roused up a herd of javelina pigs that were beddin' down somewhere around here. They come bulgin' out of the brush and ran right between the horses' legs. The blasted critters scattered in every direction and hightailed. Knocked me down, and an infernal pig kicked me in the nose. I tried to fork that blue devil and go after 'em, but he nigh to chewed my arm off."

The sheriff swore louder than the horse watcher, and fairly danced with rage.

"Smoke won't let anybody but me mount him," Vane said as he swung into the saddle. "Cool down. I'll get the horses." He sped up the canyon, reloading his guns. He found the panicked horses standing quietly enough some distance out on the rangeland. He had no difficulty rounding them up and driving them back to their owners.

"Let's go," he told the owners. "But I'm scared they got a head start on us, and it'll be plumb dark in another ten minutes. Anybody bad hurt?"

Nobody was, the man with the bullet-punctured arm having suffered the most serious casualty.

"We threw 'em off balance," Vane remarked as the posse got under way. "They didn't know what they were shooting at. What light there was came from behind us and was in their eyes. I think we nicked a couple anyhow. Pull up and let's nose around behind those rocks on the chance one didn't get away. We can't catch the others tonight."

But a thorough search behind the rocks produced no bodies. Eventually all the owlhoot had made good their escape.

Sheriff Hilton shook both fists in the air. "Dry-gulch a peace officer's posse!" he stormed. "What's this section comin' to, anyhow? Those blasted railroads! Everything was peaceful hereabouts till they come along!" He turned to Vane.

"Mighty lucky for us you were along, son," he said. "If you hadn't spotted that lookout up top the slope, heaven knows what would have happened."

"They don't waste any time trying to even up a score in this section," Vane replied. To himself he added grimly, the chances were *nothing* would have happened if I hadn't been along.

There was no doubt in the Desert Rider's mind but that the drygulching had been primarily aimed at himself.

CHAPTER V

Sanders seethed with indignation when the posse rode into town with its pitiful burden.

"There's going to be trouble," Superintendent Barrington declared. "West of these hills, two lines are less than five miles apart. It's going to be a difficult chore to keep the outfits from tangling. But what I'd like to know is why did that bunch head south instead of north? That sure puzzled me."

It puzzled Tom Vane also. It was preposterous to think that the drygulching of the posse had been planned before or immediately after the attack on the train. Vane shrewdly and correctly deduced that someone in town had kept tabs on all that was going on and had ridden out immediately after the posse departed, to report to the owlhoots assembled in some secret hole-up.

"I'm going to hunt a place for my horse and then a bite to eat," he told the sheriff.

"Right down the alley after the first corner from my office, you'll find a stable," the sheriff said. "I keep my critters there. The feller who runs it is trustworthy and keeps close watch on the stock. Then you can cut diagonally across the street and you'll come to the Greasy Sack. They serve good chuck there, and the likker is fair to middlin'."

The livery stable proved satisfactory, and after seeing to it that all of Smoke's wants were provided for, Vane repaired to the Greasy Sack, a big combination saloon and restaurant. He found a quiet table in a corner and ordered a meal. He surveyed his surroundings with interest.

Although it was still fairly early, the Greasy Sack was already crowded. Most of the customers were typical railroad builders, rough, boisterous but seldom quarrelsome. They lined the bar, bucked the games and clumped muddy boots on the dance floor.

Scattered about was a fair sprinkling of cowhands, mostly gay young punchers out for a bust, but including occasional taciturn, hardbitten old rannies with lined faces and watchful eyes.

Vane's food arrived, and he addressed himself to it with the appetite of youth and perfect health. While he was eating, the saloon doors swung open to admit a group of new arrivals, a dozen or more in number. They immediately attracted Vane's interest.

They were keen-eyed, alert men with the healthy outdoor look of the rangeland. They wore cow country garb and to all appearance were ranch hands. But there was a subtle something about the majority of them that caused Vane to study them closely.

No fresh marks of rope and branding iron on some of those hands, I'll be willing to bet, he mused. And the way they wear those guns says they don't pack 'em as ornaments.

Two of the number he singled out for special attention. One, who dominated the group, was a slender, graceful man of perhaps thirty or a little more. Although his black coat was powdered with gray desert dust, he gave the impression of elegance. His hair was yellow and inclined to curl; his features were finely formed, almost delicate in their regularity. His eyes were of so deep a blue as to seem black. There was a hint of cold efficiency in his bearing, which was assured to the point of arrogance. Vane catalogued his as a ranch owner.

The second man was lean, hard-eyed, with sunken cheeks and a cruel gash of a mouth. The hard, suspicious eyes were never still, darting glances around the room, sliding off faces, shifting to the door, the windows. He kept close to the tall, handsome owner and talked to him from the corner of his reptilian mouth.

Superintendent Barrington entered the room, spotted Vane and came over to his table. He nodded, dropped into a vacant chair, beckoned a waiter and gave his order. He glanced about, studying the gathering.

"Plenty of business here tonight," he observed. "But then there usually is. What with the ranches, the mines and the railroad, this town is booming. Roma is beginning to get its share of the business, though, as we push farther west. See Wes Hardin and his Rocking H outfit are here tonight. A hard-looking bunch, don't you think? Especially that snake-mouthed range boss of Hardin's. Name's Barnes —Cale Barnes. He's the killer type or I'm making a big mistake. Hardin seems to be a pretty nice sort. Sure of himself, but not offensive. Gets along with everybody, even Clate Bradshaw. Showed up around here a couple of years back, I understand. Guess he sized up the situation in a hurry. Anyhow, he went to Bradshaw and asked him if it would be all right if he acquired a section of the open range to the north of Bradshaw's holdings. Guess it tickled the old shorthorn to be kowtowed to, so he didn't offer any objections and accepted Hardin."

The super laughed a little. "Another fellow came in not long ago, too," he remarked. "He didn't go to Bradshaw but proceeded to buy a chunk of state land without getting Bradshaw's okay. Bradshaw's got him in his bad books for fair. Guess the crowning insult, to Bradshaw's way of thinking, was the fact that Wade Fulton—that's the fellow's name—fenced his holdings."

"The old timers sure don't cotton to barbed wire," Vane smiled reply. "But they'll have to, sooner or later. Up in the Panhandle, for instance, they've already learned that fenced range has all the advantage. Cows can be rounded up and moved to market much faster. No cutting out to do. No combing range that doesn't belong to you. Barbed wire has come to Texas, and it's come to stay, no matter how much the old boys paw sod."

Barrington nodded sober agreement, then explained, "Here comes the whole Cross C outfit, with Bull Master heading the pack! If that big bruiser doesn't start trouble of some kind, I'm a Dutchman!"

He beckoned a waiter. "Pete," he said in low tones, "go find Sheriff Hilton and tell him to head this way, with a bunch of deputies if he can round 'em up. And tell him to see if Ron Sealy is still in town. He was down at the Alhambra a while back. He can handle Masters and the rest of those young hellions.

"Sealy is Clate Bradshaw's range boss," he explained to Vane. "He doesn't stand for too much hell raising. I can't understand why he isn't with his outfit now. Masters is his right-hand man, a top hand at ranch work but too darn quick on the trigger. I've a notion Bull really likes to fight. Nobody hereabouts has ever bested him, I understand."

Vane nodded and surveyed Bull Masters with interest. He was a giant of a man, as heavily built as Barrington and nearly as tall as Tom Vane himself. He had a square, bad-tempered face, truculent gray eyes and a jutting chin. His nose was large and covered with excrescences. He had enormous hairy hands and thick, corded wrists. The long barrel of a heavy gun tapped his thigh. A broad-brimmed "J.B." was pushed back on his bristly red hair.

The rest of the Cross C outfit, a dozen or so, were carefree-looking young punchers ready for anything, whether it be a fight, a frolic or a foot-race. Vane liked their looks. Nor did the swaggering Bull Masters appear to be a really bad sort, he decided. But liable to go off half-cocked at the slightest provocation.

The way Masters glowered at the railroad workers showed he had scant use for them. He nodded to the handsome Wes Hardin, who nodded back. Vane noticed that the Rocking H bunch had drawn away to the far end of the bar where they stood in a tight group. An expression of sardonic amusement showed on Hardin's face, and his range boss, Cale Barnes, seemed smugly satisfied with something. Vane began to wonder just what was in the wind.

The jabber of talk, that had died down upon the advent of the Cross C outfit, resumed, but cowhands and railroaders continued to regard each other askance. Remarks began to be tossed back and forth, none of them complimentary to the recipients.

"It's coming!" growled Barrington. "Looks like the Cross C came here deliberately looking for trouble."

"Appears that way," Vane admitted. "They're sure on the prod about something."

So abruptly that witnesses were never able to agree on just how it started, the row began. A brawny railroader slammed a cowboy against the bar with a swinging blow. Instantly the whole end of the room was a whirling, cursing tangle of flying fists and feet. Over went tables. Chairs were smashed to kindling wood. Their occupants, drenched with spilled whiskey and sprawled on the floor, bounced up full of fight and began swinging at all and sundry. The hanging lamps quivered to whoops and yells, the thud of blows, the clattering of broken bottles. The saloon owner bawled for order and didn't get it. The bartenders uttered soothing yelps that were not heeded. The lookouts, of which there were two, brandished their shotguns and added their voices to the tumult. Big Bull Masters was pounding away with both fists and roaring encouragement to his men.

Vane noted at once that Wes Hardin and his men were taking no part in the ruckus. They had backed away toward the end of the bar, still holding their close formation, and were intently watching the shindig. The look of amusement on Hardin's face had intensified. Cale Barnes was grinning like a pleased cat.

Barrington leaped to his feet. "I've got to stop it before somebody starts fangin'," he said. He rushed into the fray, his roaring voice sounding above the tumult as he hurled men right and left.

One of the men was Bull Masters. Masters was pretty heavy throwing even for Barrington, but as he staggered, he tripped over somebody's foot and fell against a table, taking it to the floor with him. On the table was a large bowl of steaming stew. It upended and came down squarely on Bull's red head. Bull was a mess!

The Rocking H outfit, standing well in the clear, roared with laughter. Masters went beserk with rage. He scrambled to his feet, storming curses, and jerked his gun.

Tom Vane reached Masters in a single cat-like bound. His slender fingers gripped Master's wrist and flung it up as the sox boomed. Vane wrung the gun from his hand with a wrench that nearly broke his arm.

Masters yelled louder than ever with pain and anger, and swung a crushing blow at Vane's face. Before it had travelled a foot it was blocked, and his other wrist was imprisoned.

And this time the Desert Rider wasn't fooling. Masters' yell rose to a scream of agony as the terrible grip ground his wrist bones together. He was spun around and his arm forced up behind his back till he was standing on tip toes in a frantic endeavor to ease the strain on elbow and shoulder joints.

"I'm not on the prod against you, feller," Vane told him. "I'm just trying to keep you from doing something you'd be sorry for a minute later. Now behave yourself."

What might have happened next was anybody's guess, but at that moment a diversion occurred. From the door came a wrathful bellow followed by the awesome crash of a double-barrel sawed-off shotgun.

Sheriff Hilton purposely aimed a little high, but not overly high. The battlers heard the screech of "blue whistlers" right above their heads, and felt the breath of their lethal passing. The yawning double muzzles dropped to cover them dead center as the sheriff deftly slipped in fresh cartridges. The belligerents suddenly experienced an intense yearning for peace.

The sheriff strode forward, his mustache bristling

in his scarlet face. Beside him was a small, alert man with a leathery face and twinkling black eyes that seemed to look every way at once.

"Vane, turn that horned toad loose," the sheriff ordered. "I'll take him in hand from here on. Masters, I've stood all from you I'm going to. One more yip out of you and I'll toss you in the calaboose and throw the key away. And that goes for the rest of you loco railroaders and cowhands. I'll cram the jail till the walls bulge and you'll find it awful close quarters. I'm not goin' to have riots in my bailiwick, and you can lay to it. Now get busy and straighten up the mess you've made in here."

As the subdued battlers began sheepishly to right chairs and tables, the sheriff beckoned to the fat proprietor.

"Make 'em pay for the damage they did, Warty," he said.

But the good natured saloonkeeper grinned and shook his head.

"Young fellers will be young fellers and paw sod now and then," he said. "I don't mind a few busted chairs so long as nobody got bad hurt. If it hadn't been for this big feller there," with a nod at Vane, "it might have been different. Okay, boys," he shouted to the bartenders, "drinks for everybody on the house!"

The little black-eyed man stepped up to the glowering Masters, who did not appear to enjoy his scrutiny.

"Bull, did you start this ruckus?" he asked, his voice ominously silky.

"Ron, I didn't" Masters answered. "Before I knew what was happening, I was right in the middle of things. Them damm railroaders started it. They sent word that if we showed up here, they figured to take us for a cleanin'."

"And of course you and the rest of the hellions had to come here to find out," snorted the little man, who Vane rightly deduced was Ron Sealy, the Cross C range boss. "Well, no matter what else you are, you ain't a liar, so I guess you didn't begin it. I don't want any more such goings on. What did you say, Boone?"

He turned to answer the sheriff's remark. Vane glanced toward the Rocking H bunch. Wes Hardin no longer looked amused. Cale Barnes was glowering. It appeared that neither was pleased at the turn things had taken. Vane wondered why. He turned at a touch on his arm, to face Bull Masters.

There was a twinkle in Bull's eye, and his crooked but very white teeth showed in a grin.

"Feller, you're good," he chuckled. "I ain't been manhandled like that since I told my old Dad I wouldn't do somethin'. He busted a single-tree over my head, and kicked my pants up around my neck till I had to take my belt off to breathe. No hard feelin's, I hope?" He stuck out a hairy paw.

"Maybe we can have another wring sometime," Bull remarked hopefully. "Just a friendly tussle, all in good fun."

"Maybe we can." Vane smiled. "Never can tell."

Masters chuckled. "Believe my wrist's busted," he remarked in cheerful tones. "What say, suppose you and me sit down and have a peaceful drink together. Figure I've had enough ruckusin' for one night."

Vane was agreeable, so they found a table still steady on its legs and occupied it. Masters bawled for service, which was quickly forthcoming.

The Rocking H bunch was filing out. Masters waved to them. Hardin waved back, and nodded in friendly fashion.

"A nice feller, Wes Hardin," remarked Masters. "Sort of uppity, but a nice feller. I just can't cotton to that lizard-faced range boss of his, Cale Barnes. Not that I ever knowed him to do anything out of order. I just don't cotton to him. The other boys 'pear to be all right. Keep to themselves mostly and don't poke into other folks' affairs."

"Not a bad trait," observed Vane.

"So I figure," nodded Masters. "Too many folks

are good at hornin' in where they got no business."

Ron Sealy, the sharp-eyed little Cross C range boss, had been holding an earnest conversation with Superintendent Barrington and Sheriff Hilton. Now he approached the table.

"Take a load off your feet and have a drink, Ron," Masters invited. "This here feller is—darned if I know his name, but I sure got sociable with him a little bit ago."

"Vane is the name, I believe," said Sealy; "that is, according to the sheriff. Vane, I'm Ron Sealy, Clate Bradshaw's range boss."

They shook hands. Sealy accepted a drink and sat sipping it, his quick eyes running over Vane the while.

"We can always use a top hand or two on the Cross C" Sealy said. "Barrington and the sheriff thought it was a good notion for me to sound you out."

"Nice of them," Vane answered. He did some quick thinking. The proposition was not unattractive. It would give him an excuse for hanging around, and he had a feeling that the Cross C was the focal point of the trouble building up in the section. He rolled a cigarette with the slim fingers of his left hand, regarding the range boss, who waited expectantly.

"Guess I could do worse."

"Fine!" Sealy said. "We pay a little better than average top wages for the section, and the chuck is good. You'll like the Old Man. He's crusty and holds his comb sort of high, but he's a square-shooter and backs his hands from the word go. We'll head back for the spread first thing in the morning—twenty-mile ride. Don't forget what I said, Bull—first thing in the morning. I expect everybody to be ready to ride, and I don't give a hoot how many headaches there are, you're riding. You can get a room at the Cattleman's Hotel across the street, Vane. Be seein' you."

He finished his drink and walked out. "They don't come any better than Ron," observed Masters. "The Old Man swears by him, when he ain't swearin' at him. Ron likes to get him on the prod. Nobody else has the nerve to try it, but they've been together for years and Ron can get away with anything. Yes, he's right, you'll like the Old Man, and I've a notion he'll cotton to you. Well, we'll have one more and then I guess we'd better hit the hay. Gettin' late."

CHAPTER VI

Folks used to say that Clate Bradshaw got his start at cattle raising with three cows and a bull. The cows each had twins twice a year—or maybe it was triplets three times a year. Anyhow, Bradshaw's herd grew mighty fast—mighty fast! Of course there were folks who mumbled something under their whiskers about "wet beefs" and the Rio Grande, but the chances are they were just bad-tempered gents who envied Bradshaw his three prime cows.

But that was a long time back, nigh onto forty years, and almost everybody had forgotten all about it. Maybe Bradshaw was thinking about it as he sat by a window of his big ranchhouse and gazed across his broad acres upon which grazed cows and steers and prime beef critters by the thousands and tens of thousands. Anyhow, there was a reminiscent look in his frosty blue eyes and now and then he stroked his mustache thoughtfully.

His eyes quickened with interest as he spotted a horseman riding the trail that ran past his ranch-house and curved away into the southwest. As the rider drew near, he waved his hand. A few minutes more and Ron Sealy, his foreman, rode into the yard and dismounted. Sealy nodded to the Boss, took off his hat and ran brown fingers through his upstanding grizzled hair.

"Well," rumbled Bradshaw, "how goes it?"

Sealy shrugged his sinewy shoulders. "Oh, so-so," he replied. "The boys are doin' the best they can, but cowhands ain't farmers and never will be. I figger we've sort of got things under control for the next couple of weeks, but we'll have to do better if we are to get anything like a good crop."

Bradshaw growled an oath. He cast a venomous glare to the north and to the south.

"Them darn railroads!" he spat. "Takin' over all the labor in the section with their high pay!"

"Uh-huh, they've done that, all right," Sealy agreed. "But you can't blame the oilers. They're makin' more dinero than they ever knew was in the world."

"They're just naturally no good," declared Bradshaw. "Quittin' me at this time of the year, when I need 'em worst. I always paid 'em well. None of the boys have quit to take on in them construction camps, and they could make more there than I pay 'em, too."

"There's a difference, Boss," Sealy, a fair man, replied quietly. "Cowhands are different, in the first place, and besides, you've always treated the boys as men, and they appreciate it. They'd stick by you no matter what happened."

"Don't I treat the oilers right? I pay 'em well. I provide good bunkhouses and good chuck."

"Uh-huh, you do that," Sealy admitted, "but you treat 'em as hired hands and nothin' more. You don't like 'em, and you show it. They're human bein's like the rest of us, and they got feelin's. They work for you for the money you pay 'em, and that's all."

Bradshaw glared fiercely at his foreman and swore, but he knew very well no matter what attitude he adopted toward Sealy, he never scared him and never fooled him. Abruptly he changed the subject.

"How about that new hand you hired last week?" he asked.

Sealy's keen black eyes brightened. "He's prime," he replied. "I never saw a better hand with a horse or a rope, and he knows more about the cow business than either you or I do, and that's sayin' plenty. I wish I had a dozen like him."

Bradshaw grunted and stroked his mustache. Sealy grew enthusiastic.

"He don't miss nothin'," he continued, apropos of

the puncher under discussion, "and there don't seem to be nothin' he don't know about. I had him down to the farm, of course, with the rest of the boys, for the past few days, and he's as good with a hoe or a shovel as he is with a rope. Knew just what to do all the time. We hadn't been there an hour before I found him lookin' over the irrigation system, and I saw right off he didn't approve of the way it was workin'."

"How's that?"

"Well, you know the trouble we've always had with the main outflow siltin' up where it leaves the crik? All the time, almost, there's a bunch at work dredgin' out that darn ditch. Well, the big feller looked it over, took out a little book and a pencil and did some figurin'. Then he come to me and made a suggestion. And, Boss, it's a funny thing," Sealy interrupted himself, "when that feller makes a suggestion, you get a feelin' he's givin' an order, and you also get a feelin' that no matter who you are, you're goin to take the powders from him. Oh, I know, I'm range boss and got all the say, but just the same I felt that way. Before I knowed it, I had a bunch of the boys with picks and bars and shovel and dynamite bustin' a channel through the rock wall to the west, a mite below the irrigation ditch outlet."

"Bustin' a hole in the wall!" sputtered Bradshaw.

"What good would that do? Just waste water into the canyon."

"Uh-huh, that's what I figured," Sealy admitted, "but it didn't work out that way. As soon as we opened up that channel and a lot of water went tumblin' into the canyon, that darn crik speeded up past the outlet. We get just as much water as before, but we don't get no silt to speak of. The water comes into the ditch with a rush, and what silt it brings with it is spread out through the field ditches, where it don't do no harm. Can you beat that? And neither of us ever thought of it."

"Sounds like considerable of a gent," Bradshaw agreed. "Big feller, ain't he?"

"Uh-huh, he sure is. About six-four, I figure, with shoulders wide as a barn door. Stern-lookin', too, with them long gray-green eyes and that hawk face. But he sure can look pleasant when he wants to. Got the whitest, evenest teeth I ever saw, and when he grins the corners of his mouth sort of turns up and them cold eyes get all warm and sunny, with crinkles around the outside. The boys have all took to him amazin', pertickler after what he did to Bull Masters the other evenin'."

"How's that?"

"Well, you know, Bull sort of he-wolf's it over the boys. I told you about the rukus in Sanders last week, when that feller Vane made Bull look silly. Well, Bull sort of felt that he was caught off balance that night, so he challenged Vane to a friendly wring. Reckon he won't do it again."

"What you mean?"

"That big jigger handled Bull like he was a kid, and did it so easy he made Bull look plumb foolisher than the first time."

"What you tryin' to tell me?" demanded Bradshaw. "Bull Masters is one of the strongest men in Texas!"

"Uh-huh, maybe," Sealy agreed, adding soberly, "but he sure ain't the strongest. That was proved plumb conclusive."

Bradshaw whistled. "And the jigger's a cowhand, too?"

"Prime," Sealy replied; then hesitantly, "but I got a notion he ain't worked at it over much for quite a spell."

"How you know?"

"Well, Boss, you know I don't miss much, and I got a look at that jigger's hands. There are mighty few rope or brandin' iron marks on 'em, and what there are were made a long time back. But he *has* got calluses on his thumbs and first fingers."

"Quick-draw man, eh?"

"Maybe. Anyhow, he's a two gun man, and them big Colts is slung mighty low."

Bradshaw grunted, and tugged at his mustache. "Chances are he'll drag his twine all of a sudden, a day or so before a sheriff or a Ranger shows up. Wouldn't be surprised. We're gettin' the darnedest collection of choice specimens in this section of late. The railroads are to blame. That sort follers a railroad buildin'. I wish they'd both go bust."

"Maybe they will," Sealy observed hopefully, glancing westward to where a dozen miles distant, a range of tall, craggy hills cut the skyline. "The old Chamizal Hills over there are givin' 'em plenty of trouble, and then they're fightin' each other, too. That's why they upped labor wages like they did—each tryin' to get all the workers they can away from the other one. Spendin' money like water. There must be a limit."

Bradshaw growled. He turned abruptly at the sound of hoofbeats approaching from the east. His face darkened as a group of four riders swept past the ranchhouse. Foremost was a rather tall, well set-up young man with a humorous mouth. There was a twinkle of amusement in his gray eyes as he glanced toward the stiff-backed pair in the yard. Bradshaw spat a vicous oath as the quartette drummed around a bend and out of sight.

'It sure makes me want to paw sod—that owl-hootin' hellion ridin' across my land and right past my *casa*!" he snorted. "Some day I'll put a stop to it."

"It's an open trail, Boss," Sealy cautioned. "It was an open trail before you took over hereabouts. You can't monkey with an open trail. Besides, nobody has ever proved any owlhootin' on Wade Fulton."

"If he ain't one, he will be," Bradshaw declared with conviction. "This section is gettin' so it ain't fit to live in. Killin's, hold-ups, wideloopin'! And them railroads are to blame for it all. Wonder where that bunch of hellions was headed for?"

"Roma, or Fulton's spread, I reckon," replied Sealy. "The trail runs there."

Bradshaw grunted something that was not pious. "By the way," he asked, "what was that big new hand's name? I forgot."

"Vane," Sealy replied. "Tom Vane."

CHAPTER VII

Meanwhile, the Cross C hands had left the farm and were riding north by west. Range work had been neglected for the past ten days and there were chores to do. At the head of the rollicking bunch rode Bull Masters and the man who had bested him in a friendly wring, Tom Vane.

Since coming out second best in his encounter with the new hand, Bull's attitude toward Vane resembled that of an adoring but somewhat bad-tempered Newfoundland dog for his boss. As folks said, "Bull loves a man who can lick him, but he ain't had many heartaches!"

Masters was in charge of the bunch in Sealy's absence. The chore of the moment was to check cows available for a shipping herd for which Bradshaw had an order. So it was not long before the hands were scattered over the range in groups of two or three, combing brakes and thickets, exploring canyons where fat beefs holed up to escape the heat.

Vane, mounted on his great blue moros, accompanied Masters, who forked a tall roan of speed and endurance. No roping or branding was in prospect, so most of the hands rode their pet saddle horses whose legs would not have ordinarily been risked in routine ranch work.

"Me and Vane are goin' to look over Big Bowl Canyon a little later," Bull told his men. "You jiggers can work around in that direction and we'll figure to get together south of the gulch just before sundown. Then we'll head back for the *casa* together. Okay?"

The sun was low in the west when Vane and Masters sighted the dark mouth of Big Bowl Canyon. Masters glanced dubiously at the great red orb hanging just above the western hill crests.

"What say?" he asked Vane. "Shall we amble in for a look-see? It's gettin' close to dark, but maybe we'll have time to give the place a quick once-over."

"Okay by me," Vane replied.

"Lets go then," agreed Masters, and they sent their horses toward the ominous-looking gorge.

"This is a funny place," Masters said as they entered the canyon, which was little over fifty feet in width with perpendicular rock walls and a stony floor where grew scant vegetation. "For nearly a mile she runs like this; then all of a sudden she takes a bend and right after opens into a big bowl with plenty of grass and several nice springs. Cows drift in here and hole up. The only way out except down here is a trail over the west slope that's so steep cows won't take it. They bunch up in here for fair. More than once we've got nearly a shippin' herd out of this crack."

Vane nodded, and they rode up the gorge at a swift canter. It was already shadowy between the rock walls, and the hush of evening flowed around them like an invisible stream. The click of the horses' irons on the stony soil sounded very loud and the echoes of their passing were flung back magnified and distorted. Finally, ahead, Hatfield could see where the canyon began its abrupt curve. The sun was invisible now and the cliff summits were ringed about with saffron flame, while the sky above was like an inverted bowl dripping slow fire.

"Say!" Masters exclaimed suddenly, "what's that? Sounds like thunder a long ways off."

Vane also heard it, a loudening rumble that quivered the rock walls. Abruptly he reined Smoke in.

"Easy," he cautioned Masters. "Something funny about that. Isn't any water up there that could loose a flood, is there?"

"Heck, no!" Masters replied, "just some springs.

They wouldn't—Lord almighty!"

The rumbling had become a crashing roar. Around the bend bulged a sea of tossing heads, clashing horns and wildly rolling eyes that filled the canyon from wall to wall. Above the thunder of the hoofs sounded the bleating of terrified cattle.

"A stampede!" yelled Vane. "Hightail, feller; we mustn't get caught here!"

Together they whirled their horses and tore back down-canyon, the maddened cows rolling after them in a shaggy flood.

"What in blazes set those critters off that way?" Vane wondered as Smoke's irons rang loud on the rocks. "Something funny about this."

The situation was far from pleasant. The canyon floor was cracked and split, littered with boulders and clumps of growth with protruding roots. They dared not push their horses to top speed because of the constant danger of a fall. And they had fully a mile to go before clearing the confining walls of the gorge. Behind them the herd tore along at a prodigious rate. Vane glanced over his shoulder and saw that the racing cows were gaining.

"It's going to be close!" he shouted to Masters, who rode half a length behind the speeding moros.

"And if those sons catch up with us we're done!" Masters boomed back. "They'll be all over us in a minute. Ride, feller!"

Nearer and nearer drew the mouth of the gorge, but the herd was swiftly closing the distance. Vane took a chance and spoke to Smoke. Instantly the great moros lengthened his stride. The roan thundered after him, but dropped back a little.

Vane heard a wild yell, and a crash. He whirled in the saddle. The roan was down in a scrambling heap. Master had freed himself from the stirrups in the split second of time vouchsafed him and had flung himself free. He was rolling over and over on the ground. As Vane jerked Smoke around in a floundering circle, Masters staggered to his feet, reeling drunkenly. The roan had also regained his footing. Snorting wildly, he raced past Vane, headed for the open.

Vane sent Smoke charging back into the very face of the herd.

"Up!" he roared to Masters. "Up behind me!"

He reached down, put forth every ounce of his great strength and dragged the reeling puncher onto Smoke, behind the cantle. Masters scrambled, floundered, got his legs around Smoke's barrel. Vane whirled the horse down-canyon.

But the herd was upon them. Smoke screamed with pain and rage as a horn raked his rump. He staggered sideways, almost went down under the impact of heavy bodies. Vane jerked his gun and fired left and right until the six was empty. Then he flailed madly with the heavy barrel, the steel crashing against horns and skulls. Smoke charged ahead, driving his mighty weight through the sea of flesh and bone that hemmed him in. His forward surge knocked two steers off their feet. The others rolled over them, but a second of time was gained. A final mighty bound and the moros cleared the herd and was racing ahead of the stampede.

Vane let him go. They had to chance the boulders and the fissures. It was a wild and desperate gamble, their lives depending on the moros keeping his footing. Once he hooked a hoof under a protruding root, and for a horrible instant, Vane was sure they were gone. But the blue horse regained his balance by a miracle of strength and agility. A moment later he shot from the canyon mouth, snorting wildly, with the stampeding herd thundering at his heels. Vane sent him diagonally across the prairie for some distance and then pulled him to a panting halt beside Masters' roan which stood with tossing head and flaring nostrils, still shivering with fright but evidently little the worse for his tumble.

"Feller," Masters began a trifle shakily, "if it hadn't been for you—"

"Look out!" Vane shouted. "It isn't over yet. Fork your bronk!"

From the canyon sounded a wild shouting and a stutter of shots. As the last of the steers shot from the gorge mouth like pips squeezed from an orange, on their heels come more than a dozen horsemen, shooting and yelling.

"Thought so!" cried Vane. He jerked his loaded gun and sent a stream of lead hissing toward the galloping horsemen. The triumphant yells changed to howls of alarm as one of the wideloopers whirled from the saddle. A second reeled sideways. A third, with a scream of pain, grabbed his blood-spouting arm. Masters' gun boomed and a horse went down, hurling its rider over its head like a flung stone. Then bullets screeched around Vane and Masters as the owlhoots returned the fire.

Masters urged his horse forward, but Vane gripped the roan's bit iron and jerked him around. "Ride!" he barked at the Cross C puncher. "There are too many of them."

Masters obeyed, fuming and cursing. The rustlers turned from the scattering herd and raged in pursuit. But Smoke and the roan swiftly drew away. Vane, bending low in the saddle, twisted around and studied the charging troop.

"A little farther," he told the swearing Masters, "just a little farther. We're nearly out of sixgun range now. A little more."

Another three hundred yards, and Vane jerked Smoke to a halt. He dropped to the ground, sliding his heavy Winchester from the saddle boot as he went down. The stock clamped against his shoulder, his green eyes glanced along the sights. The rifle bucked, its muzzle spouting flame and smoke.

One of the rustlers flung up his arms, toppled slowly and plunged to the ground. There was an instant of wild confusion as the others swerved their plunging horses and went racing away across the prairie, bullets from the Winchester speeding them on their way.

Vane slammed his rifle into the boot and forked Smoke. "Get goin'," he told Masters. "They'll get their own long guns into action in a minute, and they're still five to one."

But Masters let out a joyous whoop. "Here come the boys!" he bellowed. "Now we'll give 'em what for!"

Over a ridge less than a quarter of a mile distant streamed the Cross C hands. The owlhoots, now themselves outnumbered, sighted them at the same instant. They turned their horses and raced south. Vane and Masters speeded after them, but were forced to hold back somewhat until the hard-riding cowboys caught up.

"After 'em," Vane ordered. "Their horses must be

pretty well blown after pushing that herd down the canyon. We'll catch 'em up before it gets too dark."

Mile after mile they rode, with the cowhands slowly cutting down the rustlers' lead. The gloom of late evening deepened as a heavy cloudbank stole across the slant of the western sky. The gleaming twin ribbons of the railroad came into view, flowing from the mouth of a cut a hundred yards or so west of the track the outlaws followed. Beyond the railroad was broken land—sags and rises and cut-banks slashed by gulches and draws and narrow gorges.

"Got to close in on them before they make those badlands down there," Vane told the others. "If we don't, they're liable to give us the slip as it gets darker. Sift sand, you work dodgers!"

The punchers urged their horses to greater effort. Rapidly they closed the distance. The fleeing rustlers flashed across the railroad and hightailed it for the shelter beyond. Vane slid his Winchester from the boot.

"Pull up just this side of the tracks and start shooting," he directed. "They're in easy range now."

The Cross C bunch jerked their horses to a slithering stop. Guns lined sights with the wideloopers. And then disaster struck.

From the cut boomed a long material train. A line of tall boxcars bulged between the pursuers and their quarry. The wrathful cowhands, gesturing toward the escaping rustlers, bawled curses and shook their fists at the fireman who leaned out of the engine cab and stared at them. The fireman gazed in astonishment, twisting on his seatbox to look back, then ducked inside the cab.

"She'll be past in a minute," Vane shouted. "Get set, and after the hellions again."

Suddenly the booming exhaust stopped off in a swirling column of black smoke. The howl of the rising safety valve was drowned in a clang-jangling of brake rigging and the screech of brake shoes on wheels. The long train ground to a jolting stop with a portion of its length still in the cut. The engineer had evidently misinterpreted the gestures and halted his train to see what was the trouble. The way across the tracks was effectually blocked.

"Come on!" roared Vane, "around the head end!" He sent Smoke charging parallel to the right-of-way.

But the train was nearly half a mile long. When the cursing cowboys clattered across the tracks in front of the panting engine, the wideloopers had vanished.

Vane pulled up, shaking his head. "No use," he told the others. "It'll be black dark in another ten minutes. No telling which one of those cracks over there they slid into, and we can't trail them in the dark. They got the breaks, that's all. Better luck next time. Anyhow, they didn't get the cows."

"And about three of the sidewinders didn't get a break!" growled Bull Masters. "They're up there by the canyon mouth—to stay. Shall we ride back and see about 'em?"

"We'd have plenty of trouble locating them in the dark, and it's coming on to rain," Vane replied. "Reckon they'll keep till morning."

"That's right,' grunted Masters, "and I'm hungry. Let's head for home. Aw, hightail it with that darn cast-iron cayuse!" he bellowed at the engineer and foreman who were shouting questions. "Sift sand! You've caused trouble enough already. Your railroad is to blame for everything, per usual!"

CHAPTER VIII

Through a driving rain accompanied by an unpleasantly cold wind, the disgruntled punchers started on the long ride back to the Cross C ranchhouse.

Old Clate, with Ron Sealy, was up and waiting when the hands trooped into the big kitchen for a late supper. He was in far from a good temper.

"Where in blazes have you been?" he demanded. "Snuck off to town for a bender, eh? Well, listen to me, the lot of you—"

"Hold it Boss," Bull Masters broke in. "I got somethin' to tell you."

Bull told him what happened, and the tale lost nothing in the telling. When it was finished, old Clate swore till the shingles jumped on the roof. He gave Vane a nod of approbation.

"You 'pear to be considerable of a feller, son," he said. "Much obliged for savin' Bull's worthless carcass. He'll come in handy when he gets older—to render down for lard!

"You didn't happen to get a look at any of them hellions, did you?" he asked Masters.

The big puncher shook his head. "Nope," he replied, "not an over good one. I was too busy dodgin' cows and lead to pay much attention to anythin' else."

Bradshaw turned to Sealy. "You were in town this evenin', Ron," he remarked. "Happen to notice Wade Fulton while you was up there?"

"Nope, I didn't," Sealy replied, "but I wasn't every place in town."

"In the Ace Full?"

"Uh-huh."

"The Four Deuces?"

"I was there, too."

"The Alhambra?"

"That's right."

"And you didn't notice Fulton in any of 'em— the chief cowhand hangouts in town."

"Look here, Boss," replied Sealy, 'I know what you're aimin' at. You can't accuse Fulton of havin' part in that wideloopin' just because I didn't happen to see him in Roma this evenin'. That's goin' a mite too far, even if you don't like the jigger, and you know it."

Old Clate growled, and tugged his mustache. The Cross C hands glanced uncomfortably at one another. Vane spoke for the first time.

"I'm sort of new here, suh," he observed deferentially. "Just who is this Fulton feller you're talking about?"

"He's a nester, if he ain't worse," growled Bradshaw.

"Hold it, Boss," interpolated Sealy. "He got title to his land. Paid for it."

"He didn't have no business gettin' title to it!" bawled Bradshaw. "That section was always open range, and you know it. Fencin' open range!"

"I'd say he isn't any more of a nester than Wes Hardin, and you think purty well of Hardin," Sealy observed.

"Hardin's different," declared Bradshaw. "He come to me fust off and asked if he could run his herd onto the northwest rangeland; asked the other fellers, too. Hardin works with us and does things like we do. He don't fence his range, like Fulton. Fencin' open range!"

There was a mocking light in Sealy's eyes as he twinkled them at the Boss. He had the look, Vane thought, of a man who knows a good joke but isn't quite ready to tell it. He chuckled as he replied:

"Uh-huh, Fulton says that's the only way to handle

THE DESERT RIDER 91

cows nowadays, and I notice he has his beefs headed
for market while the rest of us are still cuttin' out
and brandin' at the roundup."

"That's right; he ships cows to market, too darn
many of 'em!" Bradshaw returned grimly.

Sealy, who evidently liked to get the Boss riled,
winked at Vane and was about to renew the assault
when Bull Masters hurriedly broke in to change the
topic of conversation and restore peace.

"Boss," Bull said, "if you don't mind, Vane and
me would like to ride up to Big Bowl Canyon first
thing in the mornin' and look them jiggers over.
Figger we might recognize some of 'em."

"Uh-huh," Bradshaw nodded, "I wouldn't be a
mite surprised if you do. Sure hope you spot one
in particular; not that I'm expectin' any such luck.
Go ahead. And you, Ron, you head for town in
the mornin' and notify the sheriff and the coroner.
Reckon they'll want to look 'em over, too. Now all
of you hit the hay as soon as you eat your supper.
We got work to do."

Vane and Masters headed for Big Bowl Canyon
the following morning as soon as breakfast was over.
Masters seemed preoccupied and not his usual boisterous self.

"Sealy likes to get the Old Man worked up," he
remarked suddenly. "They've knowed each other for

better'n thirty years. But I wish he'd lay off Wade Fulton—the Old Man, I mean. That kind of talk sooner or later means trouble. I know Fulton fenced his range, and bought up a mighty nice section under the Old Man's nose, but nobody has ever proved anything off-trail against him."

"What do you think of him?" Vane asked.

Masters looked uncomfortable. "Well, I don't know," he admitted. "Wade is a funny sort of a jigger, kind of uppity. Nobody knows anything much about him, and he don't talk over much about himself. Come from up in the Panhandle, I've heard, just exactly where nobody seems to know. He knows the cow business, and he's got a hard bunch ridin' for him. 'Pears to be a educated sort of feller. Don't mix much. He riled the Old Man and the rest of the old-timers hereabouts for fair when he bought that land from the state."

"Bradshaw doesn't own his range, then?"

"He own some," Masters replied. "All this section, and where the ranchhouse is, and over past the farm, and clear south to town. But the north and east grazin' is still open range. Him and the Walkin' R and the Tree L and the Flyin' V and Wes Hardin's Rockin' H graze that section together. They all get along. As I told you in Sanders, Hardin is a plumb nice feller. Come here about a year back, from over in the Nueces country. Had letters from folks over there, and good bank references. Was runnin' his herd west. Stopped off and had a talk with the Old Man. Bradshaw took to him first off. Ended up by invitin' him to squat here. Hardin sure has a talkin' way with him. Gets along with everybody and everybody likes him. Fine feller, all right, and I've a notion him and the Old Man will end up closer together than ever now."

"How's that?"

"Well, I've a notion Hardin is sort of sweet on Miss Pat, the Old Man's gal. Anyhow, he hangs around a lot."

"Bradshaw has a daughter, then?"

"That's right. She's been visitin' over East for the past month. Reckon she's due back most any day now. She's a fine gal, a ridin', shootin' tomboy sort with big blue eyes and the purtiest yaller curls you ever saw. Just turned twenty-one. I've a notion you'd take a shine to her yourself, Tom. Maybe you might give Wes Hardin a run for his dinero. Miss Pat seems to like 'em big. Hardin ain't quite as tall as you, but I've a notion he weighs more. Mighty wide in the shoulders."

Vane smiled slightly and changed the subject. "There's the canyon," he remarked. "We ought to be there in another ten minutes."

As they drew near the narrow gorge, Vane's eyes narrowed with interest. A few minutes later, Masters observed what Van had already noticed.

"Say!" he exclaimed. "I don't see those hellions!"

"And I've a notion you won't," Vane replied. "Because they're not there."

Masters swore in blank amazement. "How—what —where—" he sputtered.

"I'd say," Vane interrupted, speaking slowly and thoughtfully, "that somebody or other wanted to make sure nobody would get a close look at them."

"You mean somebody packed 'em away from here?"

"Well," Vane replied, "from the looks of them last night, I've a notion it's pretty safe to bet they didn't walk away by themselves. But let's range around a bit to make sure."

Masters glared in every direction as they covered the ground for some distance around the canyon mouth, and entered the gorge itself, but Vane appeared to be directing more attention to the ground over which they rode. There was nothing to be seen. The bodies of the slain wideloopers had vanished.

Vane led the way from the canyon. Outside, he slipped from the saddle and walked about, his eyes fixed on the ground. Abruptly he squatted at a spot where the grass was sparse.

"Thought so," he remarked, pointing.

Masters slid down and glared at what the Desert Rider indicated—the print of a boot-heel driven deep in the soft earth.

"Made by a jigger packing a heavy load," Vane remarked. "You can see the heel went in clear to the instep of the sole. That wouldn't have happened to a man just walking about. Here's where he heaved a body up to somebody in a saddle to pack away."

"But who could it have been?" demanded Masters.

"That remains to be found out," Vane told him, "but I figure you can be safe in betting that the jiggers we chased across the railroad last night slid back here later and picked up the bodies. Either that or somebody was keeping tabs all the time on what was going on. That's not likely, though, for if they had been, we would have been mighty liable to have stopped some lead yesterday evening. Anybody watching would have been holed up and in prime postion for a mite of fancy drygulching."

"Reckon that's right," Masters agreed. "Now what are we to do?"

"I figure we'd better ride for the trail and try and catch Sealy, or anyhow head off the sheriff and the coroner," Vane replied. "No sense in them riding way up here for nothing."

"That's a notion, all right," agreed Masters. "Let's go!"

They sent their horses southward and slightly to the west at a fast pace. The trail was empty when they reached it, so they headed around the long southerly curve for town. On either side the treeless prairie rolled, practically devoid of vegetation except for the rich carpet of grass. Masters suddenly shielded his eyes with his hand and gazed ahead.

"What's that layin' on the trail there?" he asked.

"It's a man, or what's left of him," Vane replied, "I don't like the way he's lying."

They touched up their horses and a few minutes later dismounted beside the body, which lay on its face, arms wide-flung.

"Good God!" exclaimed Masters, "it's Ron Sealy."

CHAPTER IX

It was the Cross C foreman, all right. He had been shot through the head. Masters, quivering in every limb, mumbling curses, stared down at the dead man. Vane, his hands steady, his voice quiet, but with eyes as coldly gray as windswept winter ice, squatted beside what was left of Sealy and carefully examined his wound. Then he straightened up and searched the surrounding terrain with an all-embracing gaze. He turned to the badly shaken Masters.

"Bull," he said, "I think you'd better hustle back to the ranchhouse and tell Bradshaw of this. I'll hightail to town and notify the sheriff. I hope he isn't over to Sanders today."

"Ron was drygulched?" Masters asked.

"Well," Vane replied grimly, "I never heard of a feller shooting himself in the back of the head and then putting his gun back in the holster. Let's go!"

Vane covered the intervening ten miles at a fast clip. He rode swiftly into Roma, which was a typical border cowtown, its main street, a continuation of the trail, lined with false-fronts, every other one of which seemed to house a saloon, gambling joint or dance hall. He drew rein in front of the county jail, which also accommodated the sheriff's office, dismounted and entered the single room in front of the cells.

Sheriff Hilton was at his desk when Vane entered. With him was a big handsome man Vane instantly recognized as Wes Hardin, the Rocking H owner.

"Why, hello, Vane," the sheriff greeted him cordially. "What's on your mind?"

In a few terse sentences, Vane told Hilton what had happened. Wes Hardin sat bolt upright. The sheriff swore a bitter oath.

"Ron Sealy!" he exclaimed. "As fine a jigger as ever spit on the soil! Drygulched, you say? Just where did it happen?"

Vane told him. The sheriff rose to his feet. "I'll ride up there with you right away," he said. "Want to come along, Wes? Or did you come in on business? You haven't been here long enough to tell me."

"I rode in to attend to some chores, but I'll ride back to the Cross C with you," Hardin replied. "This will hit Bradshaw mighty hard."

The sheriff turned to Vane. "This is Wes Hardin who owns the Rockin' H to the north and west of the Cross C," he introduced Wes. "Sealy and him were good friends."

Vane acknowledged the introduction and they left the office together. "Wes," said the sheriff, "while I get my horse, you amble down and notify Doc Cooper, the coroner. Chances are he'll want to ride with us and look things over. Then we can pack poor Sealy back to the Cross C."

Masters, Clate Bradshaw and several Cross C hands were grouped around the body of Sealy when Vane and his companions arrived at the scene. Old Clate's big features looked sunken, and the lines in his face were deeper. His voice trembled when he spoke. The Cross C hands stood with lowering brows and compressed lips. Ron Sealy had been very popular with the men who worked under him.

"A plain case of snake-blooded murder," declared the old frontier doctor who was the coroner. "I'd say poor Ron never had a chance. Likely he never knew who shot him. Bullet took him squarely in the back of the head and come out through his forehead."

Vane spoke to the doctor. "Rather small calibre bullet, wouldn't you say?" he asked.

"Uh-huh, I'd say so," the coroner returned. "Sure

wasn't a forty-five. That would have blowed the whole front of his head loose when it come out. Here the comin' out hole isn't much bigger than where the slug went in."

Vane nodded, but did not comment further.

Sheriff and coroner agreed there was nothing much to do but bury Sealy. Bradshaw nodded sadly, and they packed the body back to the ranchhouse.

They buried Ron Sealy the following day in the plot above the ranchhouse where slept the wife of Clate Bradshaw's youth, and his father, and his father's father, and others. As they walked slowly back to the ranchhouse, Bradshaw dropped behind and joined Vane and Masters, who were walking together.

"Well, Bull," he said, "it looks like it's up to you to take over the chore of range boss. I sure can't depend on any other of those young hellions to handle it."

Masters flushed. He hesitated, batted his hat lower over his left eye. "Boss," he said, "I don't feel up to the chore. You know, I ain't got no book learnin', and I go off half-cocked too darn often. I know range work, but that's about all. I wouldn't be no good as a foreman and I might as well admit it."

"But who in blazes can I get?" demanded Bradshaw. "I hate to go lookin' around for a stranger. Bad enough to lose poor old Ron without bringing in some feller I don't know nothin' about."

"The man you want is walkin' right beside you," Masters returned, a touch of eagerness in his gruff voice. He gestured to his companion. "Vane will make you a prime foreman, Boss," he urged, "even a better one, I've a notion than poor old Ron."

Bradshaw halted in midstride. He looked the Desert Rider up and down as if seeing him for the first time. "By gosh, Bull," he exclaimed, "I've a notion you're right! What say, son! will you take on the chore?"

Vane let his level gaze rest on Bradshaw's face for a moment. "Yes," he said quietly, "I'll take over, if you really want me to. But I won't guarantee how long I'll stay. I'll promise you, though, that I'll stay long enough to shape up Bull here to take over when I leave. I've a feeling it won't take over much shaping, despite what he says."

"Fair enough," grunted Bradshaw. "Okay, you're in charge. Pass the word around, Bull. You can get busy pronto, and catch up with the range work. If you can do something about that farm at the same time, I won't ever forget it."

"I think I can give you a hand there, too," Vane

said. "Tomorrow, if it's okay with you, I'll take a little ride and see what I can do."

"Ride as far as you like, just so you get it done," replied Bradshaw. "And Vane, I want you to move your war-sack up to the ranchhouse. I always like to have my range boss handy. You can take the room Sealy had, if you don't mind."

Vane nodded agreement and turned off at the bunkhouse to get his effects together.

Vane left the Cross C ranchhouse the following morning with the first streak of dawn. He headed south by west, riding at a good pace. Toward mid-afternoon he sighted, on his left, the Chisos Mountains, high, multi-colored and hazy, their serrated mass cutting the southwest horizon. Misty, unreal, due to an atmospheric haze, their appearance justified their name, derived from an Apache word meaning ghostly. Blue, red, purple and yellow, they rose in a rugged wall, as if to veil an ancient mystery.

Far to the south he could see, beyond the gorge of the Rio Grande, the Carmen Mountains of Mexico, forty miles in length, with heights ranging from eight thousand to ten thousand feet. Deep, velvety red, they were as a curtain of sunset dropped to earth, but as the afternoon sunlight faded, they changed to a peculiar purplish maroon. Following the ancient

Smugglers' Trail, Vane crossed the Rio Grande. That night he made camp on the soil of Mexico.

Again he was in the saddle at the break of day. Two hours before noon, he rode into a mountain village and looked about him with the air of a man who is on familiar ground. He drew rein before a squat adobe building, dropped Smoke's split reins to the ground and entered. As he walked into the room, a white-haired man with a lined, kindly face looked up from a desk at which he was working, stared unbelievingly and then leaped to his feet with a glad cry. He rushed forward, grasped the Ranger's hand.

"*Capitan!*" he exclaimed. "This is indeed a sight for my old eyes. Whence come you?"

Vane shook hands with the old man, who was the *alcalde*—mayor— of the village. He accepted a proffered chair, sat down, and smiled across the desk at his host.

"What seek you, *Capitan?*" the *alcalde* asked, after the formalities of greeting were over.

"Men," Vane replied with a smile. "Good men to work for good wages, with good chuck and good living quarters thrown in. I can use about twenty."

"North of the Great River, *Capitan?*"

"Yes, in Texas. I can get them across the Border, all right. Do you think I can find them here?"

"*Si Capitan*, assuredly. Our young men will be proud to follow where *El Caballero de el Desierto* leads."

It was the night of the fouth day after his departure that Vane rode in to the Cross C ranchhouse. Old Clate Bradshaw was still up.

"Well," he greeted his range boss gruffly, "you sure took your time about it. Have any luck?"

"Not bad," Vane replied. "I'd like to have you ride down to the farm with me in the morning, if you don't mind, before I go out on the range."

When they rode away from the ranchhouse the following morning, old Clate wore an expression of anticipation. As they neared the fields, he suddenly stood in his stirrups and peered ahead.

"Say!" he exclaimed, "there *are* fellers workin' over there!"

"That's right," Vane replied. "Twenty good men, all real farmers. I've a notion they were on the job this morning as soon as it was light enough to see. When they rode in yesterday evening, they took one look at the fields and went up in the air. Manuel, their range boss, had plenty to say about the shape things were in. I told him the boys did the best they could but that cowhands aren't farmers. He agreed that they certainly are not."

A moment later, Vane waved his hand at a tall young Mexican who was directing operations. "Hey, Manuel," he shouted, "here's the *patron* himself, the man you're working for. He's a good man to work for, and you can depend on him to the limit. And remember, he's depending on you. Come over and shake hands with him."

The Mexican came forward, smiling, and wiping his muddy hand on his overalls. Old Clate grumbled, growled, glanced sideways at Vane. He caught the quizzical gleam in the level green eyes, growled again. Then he squared his shoulders, reached down and engulfed the Mexican's slender brown hand in his huge paw. And perhaps old Clate's ears were surprised to hear his voice saying:

"That's right, Manuel, you can depend on anything this young feller here tells you, too—to the limit!"

When they turned back to the ranchhouse after going over the fields and talking with the workers, old Clate looked like a very pleased man.

CHAPTER X

Several busy days followed, days crammed with work from daylight till sundown and after. Finally the big shipping herd was ready to roll. Early one evening, Vane rode into the ranchhouse, after assuring himself that the herd was properly guarded for the night and ready to hit the trail the following morning. As he neared the *casa,* he saw something out of the ordinary was going on. A number of the boys who had preceded him to the house were grouped in the yard, shouting and cheering, with much slapping of hats and stamping of feet. The center of attraction was a tall and rangy bay horse that was putting on as fancy an exhibition of sunfishing, high-rolling, weaving and pile-driving as could be seen in a week's riding. Vane recognized the horse instantly as a vicious outlaw that had recently been rounded up, a snake-eyed animal with a "notch in his tail," which had already killed a rider.

"Some loco hombre is hunting him a place in a graveyard," Vane growled as he quickened Smoke's pace. His mouth tightened a trifle, for he had given orders that the man-killer be let severely alone.

An instant later he swore roundly. The rider of the bay was small and slight, and Vane had sighted a ripple of flying gold under the wide hat. "A girl! Trail, Smoke!"

As the great moros surged forward, the bay went high in the air in a pile-driver. He came down with legs rigid as steel, and with unbelievable quickness shot forward and down, almost to his knees. And away went the rider!

Vane's teeth ground in his jaws as the girl's slight figure hit the grass and rolled over and over. The bay, with a scream of triumph, surged forward, teeth bared, hoofs splaying. The cowboys yelled in consternation and went for their guns.

But before one could clear leather, a great blue horse shot between the raging bay and his victim. They met shoulder to shoulder and Smoke's mighty bulk set the bay back on his haunches. At the same instant Vane left the saddle in a streaking dive. One hand gripped the bay's mane: the fingers of the other coiled about his nose like rods of nickel steel. A mighty wrench, an upward lift, and the bay's legs flew from under him. He hit the ground on his back with a thud that echoed from the tree trunks. Hand still gripping his nose, Vane held him helpless, at the same time stroking his neck and talking to him in smooth, quiet tones. A moment later both man and horse got on their feet, Vane still gripping the flowing mane. To the amazement of the rigid watchers, the bay stood motionless with hanging head.

Vane turned an ominous gaze on the cowhands. Then he cut loose on them.

"If the collective brains of the lot of you were dynamite, there wouldn't be enough to blow one nose! You ought to be playing with a string of spools! Letting a girl back this killer! One more feather-brained trick like this and you'll have something to remember!"

He turned to the girl, who had gotten to her feet and was staring at him. "And don't let me catch *you* around this horse again," he told her. "Now get up to the ranchhouse where you belong!"

The girl's blue eyes widened. "How dare you!" she gasped. "I'll ride him as often as I wish to! I won't go anywhere!"

Vane said nothing. He merely looked at her. For a moment she met the full force of the level green eyes; then abruptly her face flamed scarlet. She whirled and ran, lithe as an antelope, to the *casa*, took the veranda steps two at a time and vanished from sight through the open door.

"Come on, you," Vane ordered the bay. "Into the corral and cool off."

As he strode away, the killer ambling docilely beside him, the cowboys followed him with their eyes. Finally one broke the silence.

"Well," he said, "today I've seen two things I wouldn't have believed if somebody told me: I wouldn't have believed there was a man in Texas who could throw that horse, and I wouldn't have believed there was a man on God's green earth that could make Miss Pat do somethin' she didn't want to!"

Some time later, when old Clate Bradshaw entered the living room, he found his daughter curled up in an arm chair, gazing out the window, a pensive expression on her piquant face.

"Dad," she remarked, without turning her head, "who is that new hand—the tall one with the green eyes?"

"That," said old Clate emphatically, "is the new range boss, and when I say range boss, I mean *range boss!*"

That evening, just before supper, when old Clate introduced his new range boss, Miss Patricia favored Vane with a very cool glance. Then suddenly she smiled, and extended a sun-golden little hand.

"You were right this afternoon, and I was wrong," she said in a low, clear voice. "It was a foolhardy thing for me to do, but I was so happy to get back home, and I love to ride. I'm afraid I forget sometimes that I'm grown up."

"You haven't grown up very far," Vane replied, smiling down at her in turn, his even teeth flashing startlingly white in his bronzed face. "But it was not exactly sensible to take a chance with your life that way."

"Yes," the girl replied gravely, "and I later realized that my foolishness caused you to risk your life to save mine, which isn't nice to think about."

"Oh, it isn't hard to throw a horse when you know how," Vane deprecated his feat.

"Yes," she answered dryly, "so I gathered from what the boys had to say about it. It was so easy they're still talking about it. And when Dad heard about what happened, he gave me a talking to I'll remember awhile. I've a feeling he'll have something to say to you about it later."

"There's the cook hollerin' to 'come and get it,'" Vane changed the subject.

"And I'm starved," Patricia acquiesced. "Will you sit with me at the table?"

Just as they were sitting down to supper, the Cross

C had a visitor who rode up to the ranchhouse, called a wrangler to care for his horse and entered with the air of one who is perfectly at home on the premises. He paused at the dining room, filling the doorway with his height and bulk.

"Hello, Wes!" boomed old Clate. "Sit down and feed your tapeworm!"

Patricia also nodded, cordially enough, but it seemed to Hatfield that her voice carried an impersonal note as she greeted the new arrival.

"How are you, Mr. Hardin?"

Wes Hardin returned her greeting, casting a rather questioning glance at Vane seated beside the owner's daughter. He sat down on the opposite side of the table, at a place quickly prepared for him, and engaged old Clate in conversation which largely consisted of grunts on the ranch owner's part.

The cowboys also had little to say during the course of the meal, devoting their attention to the serious business of eating, but Vane and Patricia talked lightly together on a multitude of subjects. Wes Hardin watched them, a speculative gleam in his keen eyes, which was gradually supplanted by a rather puzzled expression.

"Haven't always been a cowhand, have you, Vane?" he asked suddenly.

"Well," the Desert Rider smiled reply, "I wasn't

born one. Had to learn it later on."

Miss Patriica made a sound that could only be defined as a suppressed giggle. Wes Hardin flushed. His firm mouth tightened. Then he smiled in turn, rather thinly.

"I just meant you talk sort of different from the way a driftin' cowhand usually does," he explained.

"Perhaps it is because I *have* done considerable drifting around," Vane replied smilingly.

Hardin nodded, and the subject was dropped.

After supper was over, Hardin lingered for a word with Clate Bradshaw. Vane passed into the living room, paused to roll a cigarette, then reached for his hat. Patricia shot him a questioning glance.

"The boys down to the bunkhouse are lining up a poker game," he told her. "I figure to sit in for a while."

"Think I'll amble down and look over a few hands myself," observed Bradshaw, who entered the room at that moment. "Want to come along, Wes?"

"I figure I'll stay here, if you don't mind," Hardin replied. "I'd like for Miss Pat to play me some music."

"Sounded as if she tried to bust the keys with that one," chuckled old Clate. "Sounded like temper to me. I've a notion she don't hanker to play for Wes tonight. Hardin is all right, though; a fine feller," he added. "He rode over to offer me his foreman to give me a hand it I needed it. 'Peared sort of surprised when I told him I'd dropped a loop on you for the chore."

Bradshaw played poker with his hands for an hour or so, then ambled off to bed.

"Want to see you in the office in the morning," he told Vane. "Bull can start the cows movin', and you can catch up with 'em later on."

The game broke up shortly before midnight, for the cowboys had be on the job at dawn. It was a beautiful moonlight night, and before going to bed, Vane walked through the grove to the edge of the trail and stood gazing across the silvered expanse of the rangeland. He turned his head at a sound. A mounted man was pacing his horse slowly along the trail from the west. As Vane watched, he drew rein a short distance below where the Ranger stood in the shadow. The moonlight beat strongly on his upturned face as he gazed toward the ranchhouse. Suddenly he waved his hand, as if in a signal, whirled his horse and rode back swiftly the way he came.

Vane turned quickly, but the foliage obscured his view of the ranchhouse. Very thoughtfully he gazed after the retreating horseman until he had vanished from sight. He was even more thoughtful as he walked slowly to the *casa* and bed. For in the stealthy rider of the night, he had recognized the young owner of the fenced Tree L spread—Wade Fulton.

CHAPTER XI

"It'll be a tough drive," Clate Bradshaw told Vane the following morning as they sat together in the ranch owner's office. Bradshaw held in his hand a sheaf of papers, which he riffled slowly as he talked.

"Uh-huh, a tough one," he repeated, "down into the corner of Presido County."

"I know the section," Vane replied. "Some good range down there, but not over well stocked."

"Just the reason why the cows are headed there," Bradshaw explained. "I sold 'em to a feller I used to know—George Godfrey—who took up land there recent. And that's why it's a mixed herd. Godfrey figures to stock his spread with good stuff instead of the spindly longhorns they got down there. Here's a tally sheet on the herd. You can check it with Godfrey when you get there ag'in' possible losses on the way. He'll pay on delivery for what he gets."

"He'll get what we leave here with, or mighty close to it," Vane promised quietly.

Bradshaw nodded. "That's why I'm sending you along in charge," he replied. "A live cow is the only kind worth anythin' to a owner, somethin' too many young hellions don't figger on when they go in for rough handlin' and too fast drivin'. Ain't none too much water between here and Godfrey's place, and a little bad calculatin' can cause a big loss. Mighty bad, to get stuck in the middle of a spread of desert and have to pound the meat off the critters to reach water in time. I'm mighty glad you know somethin' about the country down there. Bull Masters has been over that route, but Bull ain't over strong on figgerin', and he's the sort that tries to do too much at a time. All right, now, we'll start on the estimates of those northern shipments. And I want to take up the matter of a herd Wes Hardin has been dickerin' for. Sealy was handlin' that chore and had all the figgers somewhere, but I can't seem to find 'em. Reckon you'll have to work things out new. It's sure fine, son, to have somebody who can help me so well with this paper work. That was poor Sealy's weakest point, and I ain't over good on it myself."

It was well past mid-morning by the time the work was finished.

"Might as well eat before you start out," Bradshaw

decided. "You can catch up with the herd before dark without any trouble. I'll tell the cook to rustle us a helpin'. Where is Pat, anyhow? I haven't seen her all mornin'. Out ridin', I reckon. I don't figger she'll tackle any more outlaws soon, though, after the callin' down you gave her. Oh, I heard all about it, what you did, and everything. I won't forget it. Any time Clate Bradshaw can do something for you, no matter what it is, I'll figger it the biggest favor you can do me to call on me pronto."

The sun was past the zenith when Vane left the *casa.* He sent Smoke south by west at a good pace. He knew the route the herd would follow. In fact, for many miles it was the only practicable route for moving cows. To the west the hills formed an unclimbable barrier even for a mounted man. To the east, beginning a few miles south of the railroad, were other hills, but with a wide stretch of semi-arid land forming a trough between the two ranges.

It was a lonely, desolate stretch of country, and Vane was surprised, on topping a rise, to see, far ahead, a single horseman speeding in the same direction. He speculated on the moving blotch.

"Just a chuck-line riding cowhand, the chances are," he mused. Nevertheless, he instinctively quickened Smoke's pace. "Just like to know who he is and what's his business down here," he told the moros.

"On a drive like this you don't want to overlook any bets."

He kept an eye out for the lone rider, but the configuration of the ground was such that he did not sight him again by the time the sun was slanting low over the western crags.

But abruptly he did sight something, something that interested him considerably. About a mile to the right, and some distance to the rear, a group of hard-riding horsemen suddenly appeared, veering from the shadow of the western hills. Vane watched them intently as they gradually drew nearer. There were some seven or eight of them, and they seemed bent on reaching the semblance of a trail that he rode. Then suddenly his interest was intensified and became decidedly personal. From the ranks of the approaching group mushroomed a puff of smoke. Even before he heard the crack of the distant rifle, a bullet whined past, altogether too close for comfort.

"Thought so," the Ranger muttered. "Now what in blazes is this all about? June along, feller; those gents seem to want to play, and eight against one is a mite too heavy odds. I'll leave this chore up to you."

Although interested, Vane was not perturbed. He had full confidence in his mount's great speed and endurance.

"We'll just keep 'em trailing along till we catch up

with the boys," he told Smoke. "Then if they feel in the notion for a mite of a wring, they can have it."

The moros drew away from the pursuers, but when he had achieved a distance that put him beyond anything like accurate rifle range, Vane pulled him in until the group could just hold their own. Smoke maintained his lead but did not increase it. The pursuit came on, apparently with renewed confidence.

And then abruptly, what had been an amusing incident changed to a very serious situation. From the hills on the east appeared a second group of riders equal in number to the first. Vane found himself riding the side of a triangle, the forward point of which was the trail where the second group would reach it. There was no chance to turn aside to the west. The hills were still unclimbable. He could not hope to reach the hills to the east before the two groups converged on him. There was but one chance, and that a slim one—to beat the group from the east to the point where they would strike the trail. Even for the great moros it was practically impossible. Nevertheless, it was his one hope. His voice rang out:

"Trail, Smoke, trail!"

Instantly the blue horse extended himself. His powerful legs drove backward like steel pistons. He tossed his head, blew through his nostrils, literally poured his long body over the ground. Vane drew

his Winchester from the boot and balanced it across
the saddle in front of him. Face bleak, eyes cold as
the sun-washed granite of the hills, he watched the
hard riding group in front. The pursuit behind
quickly lost distance.

But very soon Vane saw the case was hopeless. The
horsemen to the east were fast getting into position
to block his flight. Now his only hope was to shoot
his way through their ranks, and the odds against
that were so great that the chance was hardly worth
considering. The only thing remaining was to make
a good end.

Faster and faster flashed the great blue horse, and
more and more acute became the angle between the
two fluid legs of the triangle. Vane cocked the rifle,
half raised it to his shoulder.

And then abruptly something seemed to go wrong
with the horsemen to the east. One suddenly reeled
in his saddle, clutching the horn for support. A second
threw up both hands and pitched headlong to the
ground. A third gripped his arm as if in pain, and
Vane could almost hear his yell. And then, above
the thunder of Smoke's hoofs, Vane heard the ringing crack of a rifle no great distance ahead. Instantly
he threw his own gun to his shoulder and sent a
stream of lead hissing toward the milling confusion
of the owlhoots from the east. Another man spun

from his hull to lie motionless and huddled like a bundle of old clothes. Those remaining madly reined their horse about and fled back the way they came. Vane sent a last bullet or two to speed them on their way, thrust the empty rifle back into the boot and devoted himself to riding. And at that moment a single horseman appeared from behind a clump of rock directly ahead, waved a hand to him and rode south.

Smoke quickly overhauled the lone rider. Vane, taking no chances, loosened one of his Colts in its sheath. Then, as on a somewhat similiar occasion the day before, he swore in blank amazement. Once again, he sighted beneath a wide hatbrim a mist of tossing golden curls.

"What the devil!" he roared as he surged up alongside his rescuer. "Pat Bradshaw, what are *you* doing down here!"

CHAPTER XII

Pat Bradshaw's blue eyes were dancing with laughter and excitement.

"Me? Oh, I'm just riding to join the trail herd," she called back, her voice ringing clear above the pound of the speeding hoofs, "Felt in the mood for a trip into new country—never been down this way before."

For a moment even the Desert Rider, who was seldom at a loss for words, was speechless.

"Of all the loco things to do!" he raged at her, when he finally recov red his voice. "As if I didn't have enough trouble on my hands without having you to add to them!"

"I came in rather handy a few moments back," Patricia replied demurely.

Vane could find no words with which to refute the statement. "But your Dad," he exclaimed at length, "will be worried loco when you don't show up."

"Oh, I told him I was going," the girl replied, "that is, I left a note where he'll find it when he goes up to his room."

Vane said something under his breath that was certainly not meant for a lady's ears. Then he threw out his hands resignedly. Patricia shot him a glance that was somewhat disconcerting even to a Texas Ranger, and suddenly Tom Vane, who made no slips when laying down the law to salty owlhoots or when testifying before juries, found himself saying:

"Well, I'll have to admit I'm sort of glad you're here!"

A moment later Vane glanced over his shoulder. The pursuit was nowhere in sight. He slackened Smoke's pace.

"Reckon we don't have to worry about those jiggers any more," he told the girl. "I've a notion they got more than they were looking for. Besides, we should catch up with the herd any time now. How come you showed like you did, just at the right moment?"

"I heard the shooting," Patricia replied. "I was curious and rode back up the slope to that clump of rocks to find out what it was all about. When I saw what was going on, I knew it must be you, even before I recognized Smoke, so I figured a little diversion would be in order."

"You created one, all right," Vane told her emphatically. "Also some work for the coroner, if there happened to be one down here."

The girl's eyes darkened and she lost her smile. "I never shot anybody before," she said, her voice quivering a little.

"You started out at a good time," Vane assured her. "I was beginning to think I was due to take the Big Jump."

"But what was it all about?" she asked. "Why were those men trying to kill you?"

Vane shrugged his broad shoulders. "Hard to tell," he replied. "Might have taken me for somebody else, or might have had robbery in mind."

"It doesn't look reasonable," the girl returned in a perplexed voice. "Why should more than a dozen men try to rob a lone cowhand who, chances are, wouldn't have more than a few dollars on him. It looks to me like somebody holds a grudge against you, but who could it be, unless—"

She did not continue the conjecture, and abruptly there was a look of pain and worry in her blue eyes, and it seemed to Vane that her red lips whitened a little. He gazed at her curiously, but as she remained silent, he thought it best not to pursue the conversation. A moment later, he stood in his stirrups and pointed ahead to where a cloud of dust rose through the dying sunlight.

"There's the herd," he exclaimed. "And I reckon they're headed for that creek you can see about a mile ahead of them. They'll bed down there tonight. Let's go!"

They quickened their pace and soon come up with the tired cows. The cowboys riding drag recognized them and waved a greeting.

"The chuck wagon and the remuda have gone on ahead," one told Vane. "Bull figgers to make camp on the crik bank. He scouted it and rode back to give us our powders. He's gone ahead again now."

They skirted the herd, passing the flank and swing riders and finally the point men who rode near the head of the marching cows and directed their course. None of the hands seemed particularly surprised at the presence of the Boss's daughter. As Bull Masters later told Vane:

"She's liable to do anything she wants to, and the Lord only knows what she's liable to want to do!"

The creek bank and vicinity provided a very good camp and bedding down site. Vane posted a double guard of night riders. He took Masters aside and acquainted him with what happened on the trail.

Bull swore with vividness and force.

"But why would they be so anxious to down you?" Masters asked.

"Well," Vane replied, "if somebody in the bunch had the lowdown on what is going on, knew that I pack the tally sheets and the letter from Bradshaw to Godfrey, cashing me in might be considerable to their advantage. Don't forget, a bunch that will drygulch one man wouldn't be past drygulching a dozen. If they'd put that one over back there, you jiggers might have woke up with coal shovels in your hands. With everybody out of the way, and in possession of the tally sheets and the letter, they could run the herd to Godfrey's place, pose as the Cross C bunch delivering it—Godfrey would have no way in knowing it wasn't so—and collect from him. This herd is worth a lot of dinero, Bull. There are nearly three thousand head, all picked stock, and Godfrey is paying top prices. Then after they had collected from him, it wouldn't be much of a chore to wideloop the herd a second time and run it down to Mexico or some place else and collect again. It would be worth the while of any widelooping bunch to try it."

Masters nodded and swore some more. "Let 'em try it," he growled. "We'll be ready for 'em."

"Yes," Vane agreed, "but it's up to us to keep our eyes skun. That's liable to be a bunch with plenty of savvy, and if they try something, I figure it will be sort of out of the ordinary. I wish I knew the country between here and Godfrey's place better. Down where he hangs out, according to what Bradshaw told me, I'm familiar with the section, but I don't know much about it between here and Presido County."

"I don't either," Masters admitted. "I got enough of a general notion about the route we're following to make it, but I'd feel better if I knew all the cracks and holes. It's a bad section, Vane."

The Desert Rider nodded soberly. "Yes, 'most anything is liable to happen down here, and usually does. Well, we won't worry about things till they do happen."

In the morning, contrary to usual procedure, Vane and Masters rode in front of the herd with the lead cows no great distance behind them.

"You see," Vane explained to Masters, "I figure if that bunch is keeping tabs on us, they'll have a jigger riding out in front. Maybe we can catch sight of him, and if we do, well know for sure they really are cooking up something."

Patricia wanted to accompany them, but Vane sternly forbade it.

"You insisted on coming along with the drive," he told her. "All right, you're here, but remember, you are just as much under my orders as any other hand. Get back and ride drag with Chuck and Harley. It will do you good to eat a little dust."

Masters gave Vane a startled glance, but Miss Patricia's only reply was a meek, "Okay, Tom," which left Bull speechless.

To the left of the only practicable route for the cattle was a range of low, thickly wooded hills. At first they were in the shadow, but as the sun climbed higher, light flowed over their crests like a flood, gleaming on the leaves, causing the cliffs and spires to stand out in bold relief. Vane's gaze continually searched the wooded slope. Suddenly he spoke to his companion.

"Don't turn your head," he said, "but slant your eyes toward that bend of thicket over there. I just saw the sun gleam on something. It may be only a bit of mica or a quartz outcropping, but it seemed to me it moved. Could very well be sunlight reflected from a rifle barrel."

Masters obeyed. A few minutes later he spoke in a hoarse whisper, although there was no one within possible hearing distance.

"I saw it, too, Tom, and it *is* movin'."

"Uh-huh," Vane replied quietly, "it's a jigger riding the lower slope. There it is again. Forget him, now, and keep on ambling. We've learned what we wanted to know."

Masters mopped the sweat from his face. "Think he'll take a shot at us?" he asked.

"Could be," Vane admitted, "but I don't figure he will. He'd have nothing to gain by downing us, and he'd just give the game away for fair. No, I 'low he'll just tail along all day, until he learns where we'll bed down for the night. Then he'll ride back and advise the rest of the bunch."

"You don't figger they're all over there in the brush?"

Vane shook his head. "No," he said, "a dozen men riding over there would be sure to be seen. They'd know that. The main body is well back behind us and they'll stay there. They'd figure one man can keep under cover."

"And he would have if it wasn't for your hawk eyes and your way of outthinkin' the other feller," grunted Masters. "Just the same, I ain't gettin' a bit of fun out of this trip."

It *was* nervous business, riding unconcernedly, with the unseen owlhoot pacing them within easy rifle range. If Vane's surmise was correct, they had nothing to worry about, but if he happened to be mistaken— well, Masters didn't like to think about that.

However, the day passed without incident. That night they bedded down well in the open where a spring offered a scanty supply of water. The cows were thirsty and restless, but the watchful night guard kept them under control. Vane was in the saddle most of the night. He was taking no chances on an unexpected attack. Pat wanted to ride with him, but he ordered her to stay in the chuck wagon, where he felt it was safer.

"As I rec'lect, there's a big crik ahead we'd oughta come to by noon," Masters informed Vane as they started the herd rolling in the morning.

"You'd better be right," Vane told him grimly. "If we have to go through the day without water, it isn't going to be pleasant."

Masters nodded gloomily, and darted an apprehensive glance at the hills that continued to parallel them on the left. Shortly before the sun reached the zenith, he uttered a glad shout.

"I figgered right," he exclaimed. "There's the crik a mile or so ahead. See her glint in the sun?"

Vane nodded, but the concentration furrow deepened between his black brows. There was a hard glitter to the reflecting sunlight that did not look good to the Desert Rider.

Another half-hour and they knew the worst. The creek bed was there, hemmed by rocky banks, but it was dry as a smoked herring. What reflected the sunlight was but a long streak of glittering white sand. Masters swore viciously and glared at the dreary prospect in consternation.

Vane quickened Smoke's gait. Masters kept pace with him, and a few minutes later they drew rein on the rocky bank. Masters swore some more, while Vane searched the terrain with his eyes.

All about was sandy desert, with numerous rock outcroppings. Vane rode closer to one of these and examined it. Then he turned back to the dusty creek bed.

"Mighty early for this stream to go dry," he observed. "I imagine it always does in mid-summer, but there should have been water in it very recently." He turned to his companion.

"Bull," he decided, "ride back and get the remuda and seven or eight of the boys. Bring 'em here hightailing."

Masters stared, but obeyed the order without question. Soon the wondering cowboys and the fifty odd horses that comprised the remuda galloped up to the creek bank.

"Okay," Vane told them, "throw the horses into the creek bed and skalleyhoot them up and down over the sand for half a mile or so. Keep 'em going back and forth, hard, and be sure to keep 'em moving all the time. That stuff down there is quicksandy, and otherwise they're liable to get bogged down."

The cowboys started at him as if firmly convinced

they were dealing with a lunatic. Horses bog down in
bone-dry sand! But they had learned not to question
the orders of the tall range boss, no matter how loco
they might sound. A few minutes later, the remuda
was churning clouds of dust from the creek bed.
Under the pounding hoofs, the yielding sand swayed
and bent like mushy ice.

But gradually the dust subsided as the pounding
hoofs hardened the sand. It became firm and solid.
And then, to the utter astonishment of the hands,
water began appearing on top of the sand. Soon the
hoofs were splashing in it and the punchers understood what Vane had meant when he ordered the
horses to be kept constantly on the move. The sand
beneath the water was now fluid and shifting.

Pacing along the bank, Vane watched operations.

"All right," he shouted at length, "drive 'em on
ahead and out onto the bank. Then let 'em drift
back and drink. There's plenty for everything now."

There was, and to spare. By the time the parched
herd leaders pounded up to the creek, there was a
half-mile of clear running water on a solid, safe bed
of sand.

"Well," said Bull Masters, shaking his shaggy head,
"if this don't take the shingles off the barn! I rec'lect,
when I was a little tad in Sunday school, the preacher
readin' about how Moses busted a rock in the desert

and got water. That was all right for a great hombre like Moses, but I sure never figgered to see a Texas cowhand do it."

Vane laughed. "The answer to that one," he said, "is that Moses undoubtedly possessed considerable knowledge of geology and of petrology, the science of rocks. He knew from surface indications that there was underground water close to hand, and that all he needed to get it was to provide an outlet, which he did. Right here the same conditions prevail. You'll notice the numerous stone outcroppings around here are granite. It's safe to assume that a granite bed underlies the ground at no great distance from the surface. The creek bed is based on granite, which is impervious—no water could get through it. Take a look along the bank down close to the sands. You'll see little clumps of grass and weeds, and they're green, which they wouldn't be if they couldn't get any moisture. By that I knew the creek went dry only recently and that the water that sank through the thick layer of sand was still there, held in suspension between the lower grains. The creek bed here is practically level, so the water, impeded by the sand, wouldn't drain off. When the sand was beaten down hard, the water was forced to the surface. Because of the granite bed beneath the sand, it couldn't go anywhere else. It had to come up, and there it is."

"Uh-huh," Masters commented dryly, "nothin' to it. Easy as throwin' a steer with one hand tied behind you, when you know how. That's all it ever takes for a feller to do 'most anythin'—know-how. But I've noticed mighty few folks have it."

Vane was gazing across the stream. Far to the southwest, misty with distance, he could make out a smudge of green.

"We'll let 'em fill up and rest awhile; then we'll push on," he told Masters. "I can see trees down there, and that means water. We should make it by dark. The creek here will be dry again before morning."

That afternoon Vane again spotted the pacing rider who watched the progress of the herd.

"Well, if they figger to pull somethin', they'll have to do it soon," growled Masters. "Two more days and we'll be at Godfrey's place."

Vane again got little sleep. Till the first flush of dawn turned the sky scarlet, he rode with the night hawks, alert and watchful. The continued suspense was getting on the nerves of the cowboys. They were jumpy and irritable. Vane almost wished that the owl-hoots would make their attempt and get it over with. Anything was better than the unbearable waiting.

On the fourth day out, near noon, a range of rugged hills barred the way. Dark and ominous, they rose against the southwestern sky, their upper slopes ending in crags of naked rock, a great natural wall, to all appearance, unclimbable.

"And there's only one way through," Masters said. "That's Rattlesnake Canyon, a narrow crack that looks as if it were cut there with a big knife. It's a bad-lookin' hole, but we have to take it."

Vane nodded, without comment. His brows drew together later as he eyed the dark opening in the granite wall. The canyon was less than two hundred yards in width at its mouth. He made a quick decision.

"Stay back here and keep a close eye on things," he told Masters. "Keep the herd moving, but slow. I'm riding ahead to look this hole over."

At a fast pace, Vane covered the first two miles or so. Then he slowed Smoke and rode alert and watchful. The canyon floor was sparsely covered with low brush, which thickened somewhat and increased in height as he progressed. With eyes that missed nothing, he soon discovered indubitable evidence of the recent passage of horses. Soon afterward he left the semblance of a trail and entered the growth which flanked it.

He rode ever more carefully, taking advantage of every bit of cover that offered. Several miles inside the canyon, the floor sloped steeply upward for some distance. Vane reached the summit of the ridge, riding warily, and drew Smoke in. He dismounted and stole forward on foot, pausing behind a screen of brush. Peering through the branches, he could see that the far side of the sag dropped steeply downward to a resumption of the level floor. Beyond the ridge the growth was thicker. The trail had veered to the right until it ran but a few yards from the beetling west wall of the canyon. At the foot of the sag thick growth edged in on the left, leaving only a narrow passage it was possible to negotiate.

Vane stared at the sinister gut below. "Here it is, if it's going to happen," he muttered. "No room down there for flank riding. Everybody will have to drop back and ride behind the cows, and ride all clumped together. A perfect set-up for hellions hid in that brush to the left. Men on the open trail wouldn't have a chance. Yes, this is it, I'll bet a hatful of pesos. Well, we'll see if we can arrange a mite of a surprise for those gents if they do happen to be holed up there."

He stole back to Smoke, turned his head north and rode swiftly back the way he had come. When there was some grass and a trickle of water, he halted the herd.

"Pat and the cook and the wrangler can stay here and keep an eye on the cows," he directed. "The critters are tired and won't try to stray from the grass and the water. The rest of you come with me."

At the same swift pace he led the hands back to within a short distance of the crest of the ridge. "Okay, unfork," he told them. "We're going down through the brush, well over to the left. Take it easy, and no noise. If those sidewinders *are* holed up down there and they hear us coming, it'll be us who get the surprise, and we won't relish it much."

Silently as shadows, the punchers stole through the growth. Before they were halfway down the slope, Vane suddenly held up his hand. The others heard it, too, the petulant stamp of a fly-pestered horse.

"They're there all right, the hyderphobia skunks!" Masters muttered.

"A little more to the left," Vane whispered. "The ground slopes down from the cliffs; we'll get above 'em."

At a snail's pace they proceeded, careful to displace no stone, to step on no dry stick that might snap under the pressure of a boot. The cowboys were breathing hard with excitement. Their eyes gleamed. Lips were drawn back from teeth. Hands gripped gun butts.

They reached the bottom of the sag where the trail levelled off on its southward way. The slope from the cliff face on the left favored them, and here the growth was thick. Farther down it thinned considerably, except near the trail where the brush grew in tall, close stands.

Again Vane lifted his hand. He pointed downward. Crouched behind the final screen of chaparral were a number of men, all facing toward the trail, all in attitudes of watching and listening. Vane straightened up, opened his lips to shout an order. But at that instant Bull Masters stepped on a rolling stone. He floundered, lost his balance, fell with a crackling crash. The loose stones his fall dislodged went bounding down the slope, making a prodigious racket.

CHAPTER XIII

As one man the waiting drygulchers leaped to their feet and whirled around with yelps of alarm.

"Let 'em have it!" roared Vane, jerking both guns. The gorge rocked and echoed to the roar of six-shooters.

Under the blazing volley, two of the owlhoots went down, shot to pieces. A third yelled in pain, but kept his feet. Along with the others, he dived madly into the growth and out of sight.

"After 'em!" Vane shouted, leaping forward, guns still booming.

But it took time to negotiate the boulder-studded, bushy slope. Before they reached the bottom they heard the clatter of horses' irons beating the trail southward. When they tore through the final fringe of brush and reached the trail, nobody was in sight.

"They're gone," Vane said, shoving fresh cartridges into the empty chambers of his guns, "and we can't catch up with them on foot. I figure they got a bellyful that will hold them, but we won't take any chances. Five of you fellows skin down the trail to where this gut widens out again. Stay there, and keep your eyes skun till we bring up the herd. Bull, we'll go back and take a look at the pair we downed, but first see if you can find their horses. I've a notion the others didn't waste any time taking them along."

With the remaining cowboys, he retraced his steps to where the dead owlhoots lay. One proved to be a gangling splinter of a man with a crooked nose and a bloodless gash of a mouth cutting his sallow face. The other was middle-sized, with scrubby, commonplace features.

"Ever see either of them before?" Vane asked the cowboys. There was a general shaking of heads.

Squatting beside the bodies, Vane turned out the pockets of the unsavory pair. The short man revealed nothing of significance, but a cowhide wallet taken from the hip pocket of the lanky one held something that interested the Desert Rider. It was a receipted bill for one Hearn & Bledsoe single-cinch stock saddle. The bill bore the printed legend, "Calloway's General Store, Roma, Texas."

"Found somethin'?" asked Bull Masters, who at that moment came up leading two saddled and bridled horses.

"Maybe," Vane replied. "Anyhow, it about confirms my notion that the bunch are from up around our home range. When we get back to Roma, we'll drop in on the dealer who sold this hellion a saddle. He may remember him and be able to tie him up with somebody."

"That's right," agreed Masters. "Here are the bronks. Purty good cayuses. The brands look more like a skillet of snakes than anythin' else. I never saw 'em before."

"Mexican burns, and mean nothing," Vane replied after a brief inspection. "Nothing much to go on there. But here is something. Unless one of the jiggers that got away forked the wrong horse, which isn't likely, one of these critters belongs to this hellion here who bought the saddle. He didn't use it on this trip, that's sure. Which means he left it at home."

"What good in knowin' that?" Masters asked.

"Might be plenty of good," Vane explained. "A Hearn & Bledsoe isn't a common hull. Usually a fancy job, hand-tooled and stitched and ornamented. I've seen one or two in my time. Regular showpieces. And another thing: you don't often see a center-fire rig in Texas, especially one being used by a Texas cowhand on the job. Chances are this jigger came from Arizona or the Northwest where he'd work with such a rig."

"If he ever worked," growled Masters.

"Oh, he's worked on a spread, all right, and fairly recent," Vane replied.

"How you know that, Tom?"

"Rope and iron marks on his hands," Vane replied. "Not new, but made not so long back."

"You don't miss anything, do you?" Masters grunted "But what's important about that new hull?"

"This," Vane replied. "If he left it somewhere up around Roma, somebody else may be using it. He might even have bought it for somebody else. It would be interesting to spot somebody using that saddle."

Masters agreed that was so. "Now what?" he asked.

"We'll go back and start the herd moving," Vane said. "Bring those horses along. We'll turn 'em in with the remuda, on the chance that brand they wear might be familiar to somebody down at Godfrey's or somewhere."

When the herd rolled up to where the cowboys waited below the narrow gut, they reported nothing seen or heard of the fleeing drygulchers. The remainder of the canyon was fairly wide and not heavily brushed, so with watchful scouts riding ahead, the cows were shoved on through. Beyond was open country where they had little need to fear an ambush.

"By tomorrow we'll be on ground with which I'm

familiar," Vane told Masters. "See, there's Mule Ear Mountain way down to the southeast. You can just make out the twin peaks. And almost due west is *El Solitario,* a high one, which is cut by the Presido County line."

"I'll be mighty glad when we finish this chore and get back to the Cross C," growled Masters. "I got more than a bellyful."

The setting sun was tipping the mountain crests with ruddy gold when, on the evening of the sixth day out, they rolled up to George Godfrey's brand-new ranchhouse with the herd. Godfrey, a grizzled oldster with twinkling brown eyes and a bronzed face that did not move a muscle, greeted them with enthusiasm. He glanced over the tally sheets after the herd was checked, counted and bedded down, and turned to Vane.

"Son," he said, "you're a wonder. I never saw a herd come through like this before. If Clate Bradshaw wasn't an old *amigo* of mine, I'd sure hire you away from him. I've a notion to do it anyhow."

" 'Fraid not," Vane smiled reply. "I sort of promised him I'd stay with him till Bull here is shaped up to take over the chore."

"Then you'll be with him till you trip over your whiskers," Godfrey, who knew Masters well, declared with conviction. "This dumb shorthorn couldn't learn to pour water out of a boot with directions writ on the heel!"

"I got more sense than to bed down in this country, anyhow," the injured Masters returned. "Nobody would live here except some jigger run out of a civilized section for plain horned-toad orneriness."

Godfrey's brown eyes twinkled at Vane as he took down a promising-looking bottle from a shelf.

Godfrey paid for the herd in gold, which was stowed away in the chuck wagon. He was also glad to buy the remuda horses which Bradshaw had instructed Vane to part with if the rancher wanted them.

"Think them hellions will make a try for the dinero we're packing along with us, on the way back?" Masters asked rather nervously as they headed back north again, after taking a day off to rest the horses.

"I doubt it," Vane replied. "Trying to run off a herd is one thing; tackling a hard-shooting bunch with nothing but a chuck wagon to look after is something else again. I don't figure on any trouble, but just the same we'll keep our eyes skun and take no chances. They're a salty lot, all right, and smart as a tree full of owls. And it's just because they are smart that I don't figure they'll do such a loco thing as taking another whack at us."

"Uh-huh, smart, but not smart enough," grunted

Masters. "Reckon they didn't figger on you or they wouldn't have tried it in the first place."

Old Clate Bradshaw was highly elated at the successful consummation of the drive. He complimented Vane on his handling of the chore, swore vividly over the thwarted owlhoot attempt, and gave his wayward daughter a round scolding which apparently affected her very little. A little later he did some more swearing when a young pucher came into the living room to deliver a report.

"Boss, I run the wagonload of supplies to the farm like you told me to," the puncher said. "When I drove up to the bunkhouse, there was a feller in a hard hat there talkin' to Manuel—you rec'lect Manuel, the tall young Mexican who is a sort of range boss for the oilers, the one with the funny twisted grin and the bright eyes. Well, right off I recognized the feller talkin' to Manuel for that railroad jigger who hired the other Mexicans away from you. As I pulled up, I heard Manuel say to him:

" 'Gracias Señor, for your offer, but we work for the Señor Bradshaw and he depends on us to get his crops in for him.'

"And the railroad feller said, 'But we'll pay you twice as much as old Bradshaw does. Forget him and come along.' "

"Why, the old so-and-so!" old Clate swore. "And

what did Manuel say to him?"

The cowboy chuckled. "That *was* funny," he declared. "Manuel didn't say anything for about a minute. He just looked at that feller, and all of a sudden he wasn't grinnin', and his eyes had got sort of shiny, like the blade of that knife I once saw him split the spot on an ace of spades with at thirty feet. And when he did speak, he spoke real slow and soft.

" '*Señor*, money is good, but there are other things. We have given our word to the *Señor* Bradshaw and we do not break our word!' After that, the railroad feller went away from there."

It was Bull Masters who, the following evening, brought an astounding piece of news to the bunkhouse.

"I stopped off at the farm on my way in," Bull said. "It was after work hours and the Mexicans was havin' one of them *fiestas* of theirs—playin' guitars, dancin' and singin', and drinkin' their pulque beer. And settin' in a chair in the middle of them with a mug in his hand, and havin' the time of his life, was the Old Man himself!"

CHAPTER XIV

The morning after Bull Masters stunned the bunk-house with his news, Vane rode north by west alone. As the grim battlements of the Chamizal Hills drew near he veered due north, riding but a few hundred yards east of their lower slopes, headed for the smudge of smoke fouling the northern skyline. Finally he sighted the busy scene of activity where the M & K Railroad was slashing at the granite breast of the Chamizals. A dark cut mouth yawned in the face of a cliff, which cut, Vane understood, later became a tunnel. His eyes quickened with interest as he surveyed the project. He quickly decided that the M & K organization was an able and efficient one.

There was plenty going on in and around the cut. From the opening in the hills came the chatter of drills, the pound of sledges, the puffing of derricks. A main track and three siding led up to the mouth of the bore, and a fourth siding was in process of construction. Cars of material lined the tracks. Switch engines puffed back and forth. The air quivered to the thudding of placed ties, the clang of mauls on spike heads, the grind of wrenches. Picks swung, shovels scraped where a gang prepared the grade for the forward creeping steel. The sunlight glinted on brawny muscles trickling sweat as ponderous hammers rose and fell or hefty crowbars heaved at the stubborn steel.

On a spur north of the last siding sat an elaborate car that, Vane deduced, accommodated some high official of the road. As he lounged comfortably in his saddle a few yards south of the right-of-way, a man descended the steps of the gleaming yellow coach and headed across the track with long and springy strides. As he drew nearer, Vane saw that he was a big man, broad of shoulder, thick of chest, with an arrogant expression shadowing his bad-tempered face. His mouth was hard, his eyes brilliant. He had the look about him of an able and adroit man. There was also a hint of ruthlessness in the pulled-down corners of the thin-lipped mouth.

"A hard jigger to go up against," the Desert Rider mused. "Drives straight after what he wants, and I'd say usually gets it and doesn't worry over much if somebody gets hurt in the getting."

As the big man approached, his attention was attracted to the tall Ranger sitting astride his great blue horse. The sight apparently did not please him, for a scowl darkened his face still more. He crossed the prepared grade on which the steel was not yet placed and paused, staring at Vane. He waved a peremptory hand.

"Get away from here, cowboy!" he shouted harshly. "We don't want your kind hanging around!"

Vane bent his steady gaze on the man and surveyed him coolly.

"Folks don't always get what they want, and sometimes they get what they don't," he replied, in his deep musical voice.

The man glared and a flush rose to his cheek bones. There was a flash of white teeth as his lips drew back wolfishly.

"Why, you impudent range tramp!" he roared, and charged across the prairie. Vane did not move.

Something about the steady green eyes seemed to give the man pause. Anyhow, he pulled up sharply, within arm's length of Smoke's tall shoulder. But almost instantly his anger burst forth again.

"Turn that darn horse around and get goin'!" he snarled. He shot out his hand toward Smoke's bridle iron as he spoke.

"Look out!" Vane roared, jerking back on the

reins with all his strength, and just in time.

There was a clash of milk-white teeth bared viciously, and between the moros' jaws was a fragment of the man's coat sleeve. Vane gazed at him with narrow eyes.

"Want to lose half of your hand, you darn loco jughead?" he demanded.

The man leaped back, more than a little jolted by his narrow escape.

"Why, that blue devil!" he barked. "I'll—"

His hands dropped to the butt of the gun swinging to his hip, but before he could draw, the Desert Rider was on the ground beside him. Slim brown fingers coiled around his wrist, jerking hand and gun up and back. The man yelled in agony. The gun thudded to the ground.

Apparently without the least effort, Vane whirled him about, levering his arm up between his shoulders until he walked on painful tiptoes. Swift as a rattler's strike, Vane changed his grip. One hand fastened on the man's collar, the other on the seat of his breeches. A mighty lifting heave, with all the Desert Rider's strength behind it, and the man's bulky body flew through the air a good dozen feet. He landed in the soft muck of the newly prepared grade and lay floundering and groaning. Vane picked up the fallen gun and with a single wrench of his fingers snapped the hammer off short. He tossed the ruined weapon beside the man who was scrambling drunkenly to his feet.

"Stay up there on your right-of-way where you belong," Vane told him. "This is private property down here and we don't need your kind cluttering it up."

The man finally got erect. He was plastered with mud and there was blood on his convulsed face. He shook a furious fist at the Ranger.

"I'll see you in jail for this, see if I don't!" he bawled. He shook his fist again, whirled about and limped toward the private car. He climbed the steps rather painfully, and disappeared through the door.

The graders had stopped their work and, with awed faces, were staring at Vane.

"Cowboy," one said, "do you know who that was? That was Matthew Clemon, the Big Boss himself. He owns this railroad."

"Then he'd better stay put and look after it," Vane replied with a smile for the questioner.

The laborer shook his head and made some other remark to the effect that "nobody ever knowed Clemon to have packed a lickin' before," but Vane did not hear him. He was staring at a horseman who had ridden out of the north and was approaching the private car at a fast pace. At first it was the splendid

roan horse and his elaborate rig, which displayed un-
usualy fine hand-tooling of the leather and much
silver, that held Vane's interest. Then his eyes lifted
to the rider's face and the concentration furrow deepened between his black brows. The tall, broad and
finely set-up rider was Wes Hardin, owner of the
Rocking H, old Clate Bradshaw's friend.

Abruptly Tom Vane was sure of one thing—he did
not want Pat Bradshaw to marry Hardin.

Hardin dismounted beside the private car. He tied
his horse to a grab-iron and entered the coach. Vane
gazed after his broad back for a moment, then forked
Smoke and rode swiftly south.

Vane took another ride that night. In company
with Bull Masters he rode to Roma. When they
arrived at the cowtown they at once approached
Calloway's General Store.

"Remember anything about this?" Vane asked the
proprietor, handing him the receipted saddle bill he
had taken from the dead drygulcher in Rattlesnake
Canyon.

The old man took the bill and squinted at it
through his spectacles.

"Uh-huh," he said, "I rec'lect the feller who bought
the hull. He was a lanky, busted-nose jigger with a
funny-lookin' mouth. I rec'lect he came in after dark
one night and placed the order, and he came in after

dark when he picked up the tree."

"Know anything about him?" Vane asked.

The dealer shook his head. "Nope, didn't ask. Warn't none of my business. He paid in advance when he placed the order, and that was all I was interested in. It was a plumb fancy full stamp, all right, as you can figger from the price; one of the fanciest Hearn & Bledsoe put out, and they go in for show."

Vane thanked Calloway and left the store.

"Cold trail, eh?" commented Masters.

Vane did not reply at once. Then he made a remark that puzzled Masters.

"Bull," he said slowly, "the cinch strap of a center-fire hull is plenty long enough to hang a man!"

Masters looked bewildered, but Vane did not amplify the remark. Instead, he asked a question:

"Bull, remember the ruckus that night in the Greasy Sack at Sanders?"

"I ain't apt to forget it," grunted Bull, tentatively rubbing his wrist, as if it still ached. "Why?"

"That night," Vane returned slowly, "you told Ron Sealy that the railroaders had sent word that if the Cross C outfit showed up at the Greasy Sack they were due to be taken for a cleaning. Just who brought that word to you?"

Masters flushed a little. "Well," he admitted, "they

didn't exactly send word. Wes Hardin heard 'em talking about what they had in mind and felt I ought to know about it. Said he didn't want to see us fellers caught off balance. He said he thought the whole business was a lot of sheep-dip, but that they were sure makin' big medicine. He said he figured it was best for us to stay away from the Greasy Sack, that we might bite off a bit more than we could chaw."

Vaned smiled a little. "And that didn't set over well with you, eh?"

"You're darn right it didn't," Masters grumbled. "'I don't go lookin' for fights, but I don't like to have folks intimatin' that I'm scairt of one."

Vane nodded, but did not comment further.

It was late when they got back to the ranch-house. Masters at once tumbled off to bed, but Vane walked to the edge of the grove and for some time stood staring across the star-burned rangeland, his eyes dark with thought. He was rolling a cigarette when abruptly he paused, the unfinished brain tablet between his fingers. To his ears had come a faint and muffled thudding, the beat of a horse's irons on the grass-grown prairie. A moment later a dark shadow drifted into view for an instant, then vanished from sight behind a nearby clump of thicket beyond the trail.

For several minutes there was silence. Then a man stole from the thicket, crossed the trail and moved toward the ranchhouse, which was dark save for a single gleam of light shining through the shuttered window of the living room.

Silent as a wraith, Vane followed. The man reached the veranda steps, hesitated, then mounted them. Vane saw his hand reach for the door knob.

The Desert Rider went up the steps and across the veranda in a bound. His gun muzzle jammed against the night prowler's back.

"Up!" he ordered in low tones.

With a startled gasp the man obeyed, raising his hands shoulder high. He twisted his head slightly, a beam from a defective shutter fell on his face, and Vane recognized Wade Fulton.

"Hold it," he directed. "Don't try anything, if you don't want your backbone blown through your belt buckle."

Cautiously he reached around Fulton's body, turned the knob and flung the door open.

"Inside," he ordered, narrowing his eyes to the soft glow of a shaded lamp.

There was a low exclamation and Patricia Bradshaw sprang from the chair in which she had been sitting, one little hand clenched against her red mouth. Then she recognized Vane and cried out in relief.

"Shut the door, Tom," she said. "It's all right. I was expecting him."

Vane stared at her. Then mechanically he obeyed. He glanced back at her as the door swung shut. There was the suspicion of a dimple at the corner of her mouth and her eyes were dancing. He glanced at Fulton who, somewhat recovered from his fright, was grinning boyishly. A great light dawned on the Desert Rider. He holstered his gun, glanced from one to the other, his own eyes suddenly aglow with laughter.

"So," he chuckled, with perfect understanding. "That's how it is, eh? This is why you snuk up the other night and waved at the ranchhouse, Fulton?"

"Uh-huh," Fulton admitted. "I was just sayin' goodnight to her."

"You see, Tom, it was like this," Patricia broke in. "Wade and I met quite a while back and—"

"And fell in love with one another," Vane completed for her. "Well, that's happened to folks before now, and the chances are it will happen again."

"And Dad doesn't like Wade," Pat added.

"So I gathered, once or twice," Vane agreed dryly.

"There is no reason why he shouldn't," Patricia declared. "It has made it terribly hard for us. I wanted to tell you about it, Tom, because you always seem to know just what's the right thing to do. In fact, I resolved to tell you tomorrow. I feel sure, somehow, that you can help us."

Vane sat down and proceeded to roll a cigarette. He looked very pleased indeed. And he was. Suddenly something that had been giving him considerable concern was satisfactorily cleared up. In fact, the Desert Rider was much nearer the solution of the mystery that had been plaguing the Chamizal rangeland.

At that moment a clatter of hoofs sounded on the drive outside the ranchhouse.

Patricia sprang to her feet, looking more than a little scared. "Good gracious!" she exclaimed. "That'll be Dad, and I was sure he wouldn't be back before morning. He planned to stay in town for the night."

Fulton also left his chair and glanced wildly about as a heavy step sounded on the veranda. Vane alone remained calm.

"Sit down," he told them. "I'll handle this. The Old Man always barks a mite harder than he bites."

They obeyed, perching gingerly on the edges of their chairs. The door opened and Clate Bradshaw stepped into the room. He blinked in the light, glanced about, and his face was something to remember. He glared at Wade Fulton, who met his hot gaze manfully.

"What in blazes are *you* doin here?" Bradshaw demanded. "Why you impudent young whippersnapper! I'll—I'll—"

Vane's cool voice broke in on his tirade. "Hold it," the Desert Rider said. "Take it easy, Bradshaw. Sit down and cool down. You'll go off in a spell like that some day. Sit down, I say!"

Bradshaw transferred his glare to his range boss. He swelled until Vane thought there was danger of his bursting. But something in the steady gaze of the long green eyes that held his was disconcerting. Bradshaw felt he should assert his authority, but somehow this tall range boss of his appeared to have usurped all the authority in sight. He continued to glare at Vane, but—he sat down!

"That's better," the Desert Rider said. "Here, have a cigarette. Tobacco is good for proddy gents like you."

Mechanically, Bradshaw took the cigarette Vane rolled and handed him. He puffed so viciously that the smoke boiled up as from the exhaust of a locomotive.

"Say," he demanded at length, "just what is this all about, anyhow? What's that nester doin' here in my house?"

"Oh, it's nothing much," Vane returned. "These young people want to get married, that's all."

Bradshaw hopped as if he'd discovered he was sitting on a sidewinder.

"What!" he bellowed. "That jigger marry *my*

daughter! Why—why—"

Vane held up his hand to still the explosion. Old Clate subsided.

"Bradshaw," Vane asked suddenly, "this little girl of yours had a mother, didn't she?"

Old Clate started. "Why—why—" he replied slowly, "yes, she did."

His hard eyes had suddenly softtened. They wandered about the room, centered on his daughter's face. Vane saw that his stern old mouth had become wonderfully sweet and tender.

"And I've a notion," Vane said, "that she was a heap like Pat here, wasn't she?"

"Yes," Bradshaw returned, even more slowly, "she was, a heap like her. Had her big blue eyes and her yaller hair, and she was little, like Pat."

Vane nodded. "And," he pursued, "she was happy with you, wasn't she?"

"Well, if she wasn't, she sure never showed it," Bradshaw admitted.

"She was happy, all right," Vane asserted with conviction. "And I've a notion, Bradshaw, that you weren't over much of bargain in those days. Right?"

"That's right," admitted old Clate. "We didn't have much, Vane. We both had to work almighty hard, but we got along."

"Yes," Vane repeated softly, and his strange-colored

eyes were all kindness and understanding. "You got along. You worked together, strove together, accomplished together, joyed and sorrowed together, and were happy. Now, Bradshaw, don't you figure that her daughter has a right to happiness, too? Don't you figure her daughter can be trusted to pick the man she can be happy with, with whom she can work, and joy, and sorrow, and strive, and accomplish?"

Old Clate tugged his mustache, scowled, glanced from his daughter to Wade Fulton and back again. Suddenly he grinned, and his face was almost as boyish as Fulton's.

"Vane," he chuckled, "as I told you once before, you're a hard man to talk to. I reckon you always get your way with folks—you're that kind—because you're always right."

He levered his bulk out of the chair, strode across to Wade Fulton and stuck out his hand.

"Okay, son," he said, "you can have her. Only— be good to her!"

He turned away, his frosty blue eyes misty.

Vane threw a long arm around the old man's shoulders. "Come on, pardner," he said, "let's you and me take a walk."

They went out under the stars together, leaving happiness behind them.

CHAPTER XV

It was some time later that Wade Fulton left the Cross C ranchhouse. He walked across to the thicket where his horse was tethered, gaily humming a tune. When he rode onto the trail, another horseman moved out of the shadows and joined him.

"Vane," he exclaimed joyously. "Say, feller, I sure wanted to see you. I want to thank you for all you did for us. I—"

"Never mind that," Vane interrupted. "I want to talk to you, Fulton, talk mighty serious. I don't want you to ride over to the Cross C alone at night any more. I don't want you to ride anywhere alone. Always have somebody with you. Two or three some-bodies would be better."

"What in blazes?" exclaimed the astounded ranch owner. "What you gettin' at, Vane?"

"This," the Ranger told him. "You are in danger—

deadly danger. If somebody gets half a chance at you, you'll get the same as poor Ron Sealy got."

"But why?" gasped the thoroughly alarmed Fulton. "Who would want to do me in? I know the big spread owners don't care much for me, but I'm sure for certain none of 'em would want to cash me in any more that Bradshaw would have. They ain't that sort."

"No," Vane agreed soberly, "*they* are not that sort, but there are others. I can't name names right now, but I'm telling you straight. If you don't think about yourself, think about the little girl you left back at the *casa* and do as I tell you."

"I'll follow your lead, no matter how loco it sounds," Fulton agreed. "I wouldn't arg'fy with you about anything, feller."

"Okay," Vane nodded. "Let's go. It's a considerable ride to your ranchhouse, I gather."

"You mean you're ridin' home with me?"

"I sure don't mean anything else," Vane returned grimly. "Let's go."

Together they rode south by west along the dark trail. The night was moonless, the sky a spangling of silver, but the prairie was shadowy and unreal. Thickets and clumps of grove had a solid appearance as if carved from blocks of ebony. A faint wind whispered through the grasses and moaned in the tree tops. Wade Fulton glanced about and shivered.

Vane's vigilance missed nothing. Continually he studied the thickets and the groves. He listened intently to all sounds—the cry of a nighthawk, the yip of a coyote, the rustle of a rodent in the grass. To Fulton it seemed that his eyes were everywhere at once.

They covered about five miles. Ahead loomed a black block of grove with the trail running through it. Vane studied it as they approached, noting that here the prairie was dotted with thickets that formed an almost solid wall of growth near the grove. Suddenly he raised his head in an attitude of listening.

An owl was whistling melodiously in a tree top ahead. Abruptly, however, the cheerful whistle changed to a querulous whine, then stilled. Vane reined Smoke in to a slow walk. His brows drew together as the bird remained silent.

"Something scared that feller," he told Fulton apropos of the owl. "Might be only a coyote or a snake on a limb, but we're not taking any chances. He stopped off mighty sudden, as if something he didn't care for was heading toward his tree. Come on."

He turned Smoke from the trail; soon they were threading their way slowly through clumps of thicket and approaching the grove from the side and some distance beyond where the trail entered it. Vane abruptly pulled up. Fulton followed his example. Together they sat their mounts and stared at the grove.

"Can't say for sure," Vane said slowly, "but I'm mighty nigh to certain that I heard a horse stomp and a bridle iron jingle. Looks sort of like somebody's holed up in there. Well, we'll have a look-see. Unfork."

Slowly and silently they stole through the hundred yards and more of thick brush till they reached the edge of the grove. Twice they heard the jingle of a bridle iron, and once there was an undoubted mutter of low voices.

Under the trees progress was easier. There was little or no undergrowth and it was very dark. Finally the trail came into view, faintly outlined in the starlight. And sitting their horses at the angle of a bend were three men. Vane's keen eyes could just make out the slim shape of rifles resting across their saddle bows.

Face set in bleak lines, eyes coldy gray, Vane drew a gun and balanced it in his hand. That the men sitting their horses only a few yards distant were conscienceless killers he felt certain. Their eyes were fixed on the bend where their intended victim would come into view. Their ready rifles proved that the victim would never have a chance. They were out for a cold-blooded murder. They richly deserved any fate that might overtake them. Vane balanced the big Colt, half raised it.

But he knew, just the same, that he couldn't do it. It was against the code of the Rangers, against his own personal code. His voice rang out:

"Elevate, you men! You're covered!"

With yelps of alarm, the men whirled in their saddles. Vane caught the glint of shifted metal and fired instantly, his gun roaring like thunder in the silent night. A thudding clang echoed the report, the clatter of something falling, and a howl of pain. Then fast hoofs beat the trail.

Half blinded by the blaze of his own gun, Vane fired two more shots, but instinctively he knew he had missed. He lowered the Colt and stood listening. The clatter of hoofs on the stony trail changed to a dull thudding swiftly dying in the distance.

"Cut away through the brush," he told the wildly excited Fulton. "Nope, they won't come back. Not tonight. But they'll make another try if they get the chance. Don't forget that. Let's see what hit the ground when I pulled trigger."

A search of the trail disclosed a rifle with a smashed stock. Vane picked it up, noted how his heavy bullet had splintered the wood.

"Went through, all right," he told Fulton. "Wouldn't have much force left, but enough to nick that gent and make him squeal."

He struck a match and examined the weapon. "Interesting," he remarked. "A .32-20. That's a calibre you don't often see in this section."

"I don't believe I ever saw one before," said Fulton. "A good gun?"

"Very good," Vane replied. "Packs a hefty wallop for a small calibre and has plenty of range. Point-blank up to about three hundred yards. A prime gun for a drygulcher who wants to hole up and take a long shot at somebody."

Fulton made a wry face. "Gives me the shivers to think about it," he admitted. "Reckon if it hadn't been for you, I'd have found out how hard that gun could hit."

"Chances are you would have," Vane admitted. "Those hellions sure weren't holed up here enjoying the scenery. Snake-blooded outfit, all right. Vicious as Gila monsters. Well, they didn't get away with it this time, and I've a notion you'll be on the lookout from now on."

"You can figger on that again, and double," Fulton declared fervently. "I won't stick my nose out unless one or two of my boys are with me."

Vane nodded. "Well, reckon we might as well be

ambling," he said. "Still got a ride ahead of us."

They returned to their horses, regained the trail and rode on. They passed Bradshaw's farm lands, skirted Roma and crossed the railroad tracks. Then they rode almost due west, paralleling the C & P right-of-way. Ahead the craggy summits of the Chamizal Hills cut the skyline, an irregular band of jet beneath the silver web of the stars. At their base, slightly to the north of Fulton's holdings, was the big construction camp the railroad was building into a permanent town to accommodate the shops, round-houses, storerooms, and other housing that had been under construction for some time, much of which had arrived at or was nearing completion.

Vane and Fulton rode mostly in silence, each busy with his own thoughts. Suddenly the latter uttered a sharp exclamation.

"Look how red the sky's gettin' ahead there," he called out. "Darned if it doesn't look like something is on fire."

Vane stared at the spreading glow which was leaping upward and brightening by the second.

"It's a fire, all right, and a big one," he agreed. "And I've a notion I know what it is. It's the railroad camp."

"You're right," exclaimed Fulton. "That's the only thing over there big enough to make such a blaze. It isn't a forest fire on the hills, that's certain, and there aren't many trees down below. Not enough, anyhow, to kick up a glare like that."

Vane's hand tightened on the reins. "Let's go," he told Fulton. "Maybe we can do something. We'd ought to make it there in fifteen minutes. Trail, Smoke!"

The great moros shot forward. Fulton's fine steel-dust kept pace.

After a few minutes of fast riding, they pounded up a long slope, topped a rise, and the scene of the conflagration lay before them and less than half a mile ahead.

A tall, gaunt structure, evidently a big storehouse of some sort, was blazing fiercely, the light from the flames making the scene as bright as day. The sprawling machine shops, office buildings, other storehouses and the great roundhouse stood out in stark relief. The firelight gleamed on the web of trackage that sprawled over a large area, funneling toward the mouth of the cut that slashed the wall of the Chamizals. Men were running about like disturbed ants. Their shouts came faintly to Vane's ears. Locomotives, their blowers roaring to keep their furnace fires at white heat, injectors wide open to constantly renew the supply in their boilers from their tanks, were pouring water on the flames by way of lines of hose coupled to their mud valves. But they might just as well have been a kid's squirt gun for all the effect they seemed likely to produce.

"The way those buildings are clumped together, the whole shebang will go up in smoke if something isn't done might soon," Vane muttered. He noted that between the blazing storehouse and the broad loom of what was undoubtedly the machine shop stood a building about the same size as the one burning, doubtless another structure intended to house machinery and supplies, and not yet completed. Flickers were already showing on its roof and smoke was wreathing from the upper window openings.

As they pounded up to the building, a big man holding a shotgun ran forward. "Hold it!" he bellowed threateningly, "We've had enough trouble around here tonight!"

"Shut up!" Vane thundered back at him. "Where's Barrington?"

The man seemed taken aback by the question. "Why, Rawhidin' Dave—he—he—Say! Aren't you the feller who stopped that runaway train?"

"Where's Barrington?" Vane repeated as, ignoring the shotgun's threat, he slid to the ground and strode forward.

"He ain't here," the man answered "He went east yesterday to meet old man Dunn. I'm Carnes, the general foreman. I'm in charge now."

"Okay, Carnes," Vane nodded. "We've got to get busy. You'll never stop that fire with water. Get dynamite—plenty of it, and caps and fuse. We'll blow that unfinished building. That may hold it, if we work fast!"

The foreman gasped audibly. His jaw sagged. "Blow the buildin'!" he repeated.

"Yes, we'll put charges under all four corners, big ones. That should scatter it all over the place. Then maybe we can hold the fire where it is. Hightail, feller; there's a wind kicking up and it's blowing from the east."

"But," sputtered Carnes, "the roof's on fire already, and there ain't no floors laid in that shack. Sparks are droppin' through. A man'll take his life in his hands to spot the powder."

"Get the stuff, I tell you," Vane shot at him. "I'll take care of spotting it. Move!"

With a muttered oath, Carnes turned and began bawling orders. Men ran in all directions. Soon they came panting back, staggering under the weight of the stout boxes they carried. Others bore coils of fuse.

"Get the boxes open," Vane directed tersely. He himself began cutting lengths of fuse, graduating the lengths with utmost nicety. He looped the cut lengths over his shoulder, gathered an armful of the greasy cylinders.

Wade Fulton stepped forward with a determined air. "I'll help," he said.

"Know anything about setting dynamite?" Vane asked.

"No, but—"

"Then there's nothing you can do. Keep in the clear. No sense taking needless chances."

"Reckon I'm hefty enough to pack an armload of that stuff," growled Fulton, suiting the action to the word. Vane glanced at him, grinned slightly and offered no further objections. Carnes also gathered up an armload of the greasy sticks of death.

"I know how to set powder," he remarked pointedly. "I'll take two corners. You take the other two."

Faces grim, the three entered the unfinished building, the roof of which was already blazing under the strengthening wind. Sparks showered over them as they groped their way into the shadowy interior. A lurid glow beat down between the joists, which were devoid of flooring. There was an ominous creaking overhead.

"She's liable to come down any minute," Carnes muttered, apropos of the burning roof.

"If she does, there'll be enough dynamite inside

to do the work," Vane replied as he headed for a far corner, Fulton at his heels.

Carnes gave a dry cackle. "Betcha a month's pay I go higher than you!" he called as he got busy in his own corner.

Vane worked with speed and efficiency, but it took time to properly cap, fuse and set the sticks. By the time he had finished the first corner, the crackle overhead had changed to an ominous roaring. Sparks were showering down ever more thickly and the air was almost unbearable.

"Now if a spark just doesn't drop onto the end of this fuse before we finish with the other corner!" Vane told Fulton as they hurried along the end wall of the building.

The whole inside of the building was now blanketed in a ruddy mist, and Vane choked and coughed as he worked feverishly on the second corner. Fulton lay flat on the ground, where there was a little more air to breathe, and passed him the sticks. All about them fell sparks and embers and flaming shingles. Their flesh was stung by the brands and some even dropped on the heap of dynamite but were displaced before they could do damage. Finally Vane straightened up and filled his lungs with the smoke-charged air.

"How about it, Carnes?" he shouted.

"All set," the foreman called back. "Time to light up?"

"I'll tend to the lighting," Vane told him, "I'm coming over to start at your corner. You hightail out and get the boys on the machine shop roof in the clear. They should be safe on the far side of the building. Then they can come ahead with their pails and douse anything that lands on the roof. Run the engines farther back on the sidings, and send everybody out of the way. I'll give you a minute; then I'll light up."

Carnes pounded out the door. A moment later his booming voice sounded above the roar of the flames. Vane waited a moment longer, then touched a match to the end of the fuse he held in his hand. There was a sputter, a spurt of smoke, then a steady shower of sparks from the burning fuse.

"Hope you didn't cut 'em too short," Fulton panted as they raced to the next corner.

"If I did, you tell me about it later," Vane replied, and stooped over the second fuse.

They were staggering, blinded, groping, as they headed for the fourth and last corner. It seemed to Vane that they had been hours making the circuit of the building. He had a horrible feeling that he must have miscalculated the time and that any second the first charge was due to let go. With trembling fingers he struck a match and applied the flame to the last fuse. Overhead sounded a mighty groaning, creaking and rending. With a crash, a section of the roof fell in. Sparks and clots of fire flew in every direction. Vane gripped the reeling Fulton by the arm and dragged him along toward where the door should be. After an eternity of effort, they reached it and lurched into the life-giving air outside. With their last bit of strength they floundered away from the blazing structure.

They were still dangerously close when the first charge let go like a clap of thunder. Then the other two in quick succession. The air was filled with flaming timbers and hurtling beams. With a deafening crash the building collapsed in smoldering ruin.

Stacks booming, the switch engines charged forward and began pouring water over the mass.

Wade Fulton scrambled to his feet from where the explosion had hurled him. He rubbed his smoke-stung eyes and swore.

"I dodged chunks of house till I'm dizzy," he declared. "You all right?"

"Reckon so," Vane replied as he also got off the ground. "One chunk caught me on the shoulder but didn't 'pear to do much damage." He massaged the bruised member and gazed thoughfully at the original site of the fire. The building had also been pretty well shattered by the explosion, and he decided there was little danger of the flames spreading farther.

Carnes, the foreman, came running up. "I was scairt you'd both be done for," he swore in great relief. "Feller, you sure did one fine chore. If it hadn't been for you, the whole shootin' match would have gone up in smoke, and if we'd lost the shops and the stores and the machinery and the round-house, we wouldn't have stood a chance at beatin' them M & K hombres through the hills. I reckon the C & P will be glad to hand you just about any-thing you ask for this night's work. Just wait till Barrington and old man Dunn hear about it!"

"How'd it catch?" Vane asked, deftly changing the subject.

Carnes swore viciously. "Didn't catch," he declared. "It was set."

"How do you know?" Vane asked.

"Three hellions snuk up on the watchman and belted him over the head with a gun barrel," Carnes explained. "He got a look at 'em, but they knocked him plumb out before he could give a yelp. They knew the lay of the land and just what to do. They grabbed his keys, got into the store buildin' and headed right up to the top floor. Up there were bins of cotton waste and cans of machine oil. They set fire to the waste, and that stuff burns like powder.

The whole top of the buildin' was blazin' in a matter of minutes. The watchman got his senses back in time to see 'em ride away. He sounded the alarm pronto, but we couldn't do much with the fire. There ain't nobody much here right now—most of the boys are in town—Saturday night bust, you know—and Barrington is away, as I told you before."

"Did the watchman get a look at those jiggers?" Vane asked.

"He said they wore masks," Carnes replied. "I ain't had time to talk to him yet. Not that there's any doubt as to who is responsible," he added grimly. "The same gang who tried to wreck that dynamite train and blow Sanders off the map; the same bunch that planted the dynamite back in the cut last week and blew two poor devils to bits. The bunch that's been causin' us all the trouble of late—that darned bunch of M & K hyderphobia skunks! But we'll even it up. We've stood all we're goin' to stand. A general housecleanin' is in order, and it's goin' to be a good one! Just you watch!"

Vane's black brows drew together, but he offered no comment.

"I'd like to talk with the watchman," he said.

"Okay, we'll go over and see him. He's in the hospital car," replied Carnes. "And I've a notion we could all stand a cup of steaming coffee about now.

Besides, if you two have got as many blisters as I have, a little salve will be in order too. Let's go!"

They found the watchman with a bandaged head, sitting up and sipping coffee. He could add but little to what the foreman had already told Vane.

"All I saw was that they wore masks and cowboy clothes," he said. "I was just roundin' the corner of the buildin' when they loomed up in front of me. Before I could reach for my gun or yelp, one of 'em batted me over the head. I was wearin' a thick cap or I reckon it would have busted my skull. All I saw next was stars and comets. When I come to and managed to stand up I heard horses' hoofs. Got a glimpse of the devils skalleyhootin' off north across the prairie, but before I could try a shot at 'em, they scooted behind a clump of rocks and out of sight. Then I realized the storehouse was on fire. By the time I got the boys roused up, the flames was shootin' out of the roof. They must have busted open oil cans and soused that waste up there with it, from the way it burned."

Vane and Fulton had several cups of coffee and attended to their burns, which though painful were slight. Then, declining an invitation to spend the night at the camp, they located their horses and headed south by west for Fulton's ranchhouse, which they reached less than an hour later.

Before going to sleep, Vane cleaned and oiled his guns. "Well," he told the big sixes, "things are beginning to tie up a mite. Eliminating Fulton as a suspect sort of helps matters. And my hunch about the trip to Godfrey's ranch was a straight one. I did manage to hit onto something that gave me a definite line on somebody. That jigger keeping that saddle receipt in his pocket was one of the little slips smart owlhoots seem to make. The little slip is liable to cause a certain smart jigger to wear a rope necktie before everything is done. Do a little work on that tomorrow."

Mid-morning found the Desert Rider in Sanders. He repaired to the railroad telegraph office and sent a message that caused the operator, sworn to secrecy by the rules of his company, to gaze at him with much interest. The message was addressed to Captain Jim McNelty, Texas Ranger Post Headquarters.

After sending the message, Vane headed back to the Cross C ranchhouse. He was working in Bradshaw's office when the old rancher entered. Bradshaw sat down and smoked until Vane had finished his chore. Then, when his range boss had a cigarette going and his chair tilted back in a comfortable position, he opened conversation.

"Son," he said, "I wouldn't be surprised if the Mexican boys over to the farm have wives and families down in *mañana* land, haven't they?"

"I've a notion most of them have, or would like to have when they're able to," Vane replied. "Why?"

"Just this," said Bradshaw. "Suppose they had good, tight little houses to live in down alongside the farm, with patches of ground to raise chickens and pigs and garden truck and so on, I was wonderin' if they wouldn't bring their families up here and settle permanent? I'd have enough chores to keep most of 'em busy all year round, and I figger I could arrange for work for the rest of 'em in Roma and on the other spreads hereabouts durin' the slack winter season. I could fix it up with the immigration authorities. And I been thinkin' the little schoolhouse in Roma could stand another room or two added to it, and I reckon we could hire another teacher or two to take care of some more kids and teach 'em how to be good Texans. What do you think?"

"I think, sir," Vane smiled, "that when it comes to having real prime notions, you're just about top of the heap."

Old Clate chuckled, his eyes sunny. "I done a lot of different things in my life," he said, "but I reckon this'll be the first time I ever built a town!"

CHAPTER XVI

Bradshaw jabbered on at a great rate, elaborating his views, making plans, while Vane offered a suggestion from time to time.

"I believe I'll ride down and have a talk with Manuel," Bradshaw observed at length. "You goin' out on the range?"

"Yes, I think I will," Vane replied. "I've about finished up here for the present." He was silent a moment; then abruptly he asked a question:

"Was Ron Sealy a native of this section, Boss?"

Bradshaw looked surprised. "Well, he'd coiled his twine here for so long, I reckon you could call him one," he replied. "But he wasn't born and brought up here. Originally he was from the Nueces country and around San Antonio. A brother of his, the only relative he had left, still lives in San Antonio. I got a letter from him the other day. I wrote him about poor Ron, of course."

Vane's eyes narrowed slightly. He looked interested. "Brother in the cow business?" he asked.

"Nope," Bradshaw replied. "He's a banker. Vice-president of one of the banks over there. Lived in town most of his life, I understand. Always been a business man in one way or another. I met him once when Ron and me made a trip over east. Nice feller. Considerably older than Ron was."

Vane nodded and looked even more interested. "They kept in touch with one another, then?"

"That's right. They were on good terms, though they never hung out much together. Ron was an outdoor jigger, a born cowman, but no business man. About all he was ever interested in was a horse and a rope and plenty of ridin' space. Uh-huh, they used to write each other. Not over frequent, but they always kept in touch. Ron always thought a lot of his brother's kids. Ron was a bachelor, you know. What got you thinkin' about poor Ron, son?"

"Oh, I was lookin' through the window, up toward the hill where Ron is," Vane evaded.

Old Clate nodded, his eyes suddenly somber as they rested on the whispering pines on the hill, beneath which Ron Sealy slept.

"Up there, or some place like it, is where we all end sooner or later," he observed. "Reckon it ain't a bad place when you get old. Well, I'm off to the farm to see Manuel."

After Bradshaw departed Vane repaired to his own room. He sat on the bed and examined the rifle he had shot from the hands of the drygulcher the night before. It was a beautiful weapon that showed signs of considerable use. It had a manufacturer's serial number, Vane noted. He considered the number's possibilities for some minutes but reluctantly dismissed it as of small significance.

"If this was a new iron, the number might be valuable in tracing it to the purchaser," he mused, "but it doesn't pack much weight with an old gun. Still, it's worth keeping in mind. One thing is sure: I'm just about certain this rifle is the same calibre as the gun that killed poor Ron Sealy. It isn't the gun that killed him, though. Sealy was downed by a sixgun, I'm sure as to that. But a .32-.20 rifle and pistol ammunition are interchangeable. And that may mean plenty."

Laying the rifle aside, he walked to the open window and stood gazing at the pines on the hill.

"Doesn't seem to make sense, at first, that a good man like Sealy would have to die out of turn like he did. But if you'll just wait long enough, a good reason for 'most anything that happens usually turns up. Sort of that way with Sealy's death.

"If Ron hadn't gotten cashed in, like as not I'd

never have gotten a line on the man who's responsible for more killings, such as that of the brakeman
and fireman and the two poor devils blown to bits
by that dynamite planted in the cut. But as it is,
I'm beginning to see a chance to tighten my loop.
The thing I need most right now is to find the hellion's hole-up, and I'm beginning to get a notion
about that. One thing sure for certain, it's not overly
far off. The way they operate proves that. And it's
somewhere to the north of here. The jiggers who
tried to do for Fulton headed north by west. According to the watchman's story last night, the three who
set the fire at the railroad camp also headed north.
And it's just about certain the widelooping bunch
we chased from Big Bowl Canyon circled around
and headed back north after they gave us the slip
down south of the railroad. They must have come
back north to pick up those bodies. At first I figured
they might be scared somebody would recognize the
bodies, but I've changed my mind as to that. I'm just
about sure, now, that it is a bunch operating strictly
under cover. And if that is so, they wouldn't worry
about tie-ups with some supposedly honest outfit here
in the section. I've a notion only the head of the pack
would be recognized by anybody hereabouts, and he
doesn't figure to be seen. The watchman said those
three last night wore masks, but that could be a

blind. Besides, there's always the chance that one or two leading members of the bunch may appear in the Boss' company, and they would cover up their faces when out on business like last night's."

For several minutes he stood gazing out the window. Abruptly he turned and headed for the barn. Soon afterward he led Smoke out, saddled and bridled.

"Feller," he told the moros as he swung into the hull, "we're going to play a hunch. Not much to base it on—only the fact that those hellions *did* pick up the bodies in the mouth of Big Bowl Canyon.

The afternoon was pretty well advanced, but Vane knew he could still count on several hours of daylight when he reached the mouth of the canyon. Without hesitation he entered the narrow gorge and rode forward at a swift pace.

A mile or so, and the canyon began to bend. Following its gradual curve, he reached the point where it opened into the bowl, which proved to be almost circular and more than a mile in diameter. The great amphitheatre, walled on all sides by cliffs and precipitous slopes, was well wooded, covered with thick grass, and showed signs of plenty of water. Relying on Bull Masters' description of the place, Vane rode straight across to the curving west wall. It did not take him long to find the spot where it was possible to negotiate the slope.

But before tackling the ascent, he rode back and forth near the base of the cliffs, studying the ground with a gaze that missed nothing. His eyes glowed as he discovered signs of the indubitable presence of horses not long before.

"And none of the boys have been up here, I'll bet on that, since we got the herd together for Godfrey," he mused. "Somebody rode this way not more than a day or two ago, maybe as late as last night. Begins to look like my hunch might be a straight one."

He studied the slope between the flanking cliffs. The trail that wound and slithered up the sag was, he decided, or at least had been, a game track. It was rough and stony, the soil packed hard, but as he sent Smoke slowly upward, he became more and more convinced that it had recently been used by other creatures than coyote, wolf and deer.

It was a tough scramble and the moros was breathing hard when at last he reached the crest. Beyond was a precipitous sag that dropped to the floor of a narrow valley, and farther beyond was the ominous barrier of the Chamizal Hills, apparently unclimbable by horse or man.

Nevertheless, Vane sent Smoke skittering down to the valley floor, which was densely grown with brush. And here the old game trail led on, winding and turning, curving around boulders and chimney rocks and leading ever westward. It crossed the valley in tortuous fashion until it apparently ended at the wall of the hills.

But Vane had already convinced himself that horses had been this way before. Straight toward what seemed an utterly insurmountable cliff he rode. He reached its base, glanced right and left, and uttered an exultant exclamation.

Invisible from the rim of the Big Bowl, because of the overlapping configuration of the cliff, was an opening in the wall, not more than a score of feet in width. Into it flowed the faint track.

Unhestitatingly, Vane entered the cleft which widened rapidly until it became more or less of a canyon winding into the heart of the hills.

Vane rode more cautiously now, listening and peering. He suffered no illusions as to what his fate would be should he come upon the owlhoots unexpectedly. He was now convinced that he was on the trail of the hidden hang-out of the band and it was possible that the bunch might be in the canyon at the moment. He glanced dubiously at the sun which was low in the west. Soon it would be behind the wall of the hills and the narrow gorge would quickly become dark. But he decided to risk the chance of night catching him in the canyon. He covered a mile and the better part of a second. And still the faint trail between the boulders and the brush wound on.

"If the hellions are in here they should be starting a fire and cooking supper mighty soon," he decided. "What little wind there is is blowing toward me, and it should carry the smell of smoke quite a ways."

The canyon was deathly still and the click of Smoke's irons rang with a disquieting loudness. There was not even a chirping of birds to greet the approaching twilight. Vane saw no signs of animal life. He did not even sight a snake or a lizard. The sinister gorge seemed to be an abode of death.

The lower rim of the sun touched the tip of a soaring crag ahead. Gradually it sank behind the spire of rock and vanished. The crag stood out black and forbidding against the flame of the sky, which swiftly became a scarlet and golden glory. In the depths the shadows were already curdling.

The canyon began to bend slightly southward. To Vane's ears came a murmur of running water. He slowed Smoke to a walk and his vigilance increased. Abruptly he pulled the sorrel to a halt. Hand gripping the butt of his rifle, he sat rigid in the saddle and stared ahead.

The trail had veered to the left until it ran not far from the south wall of the canyon. The brush had thinned somewhat but was still thick enough to afford fairly good concealment. Less than fifty feet from where he sat his horse was the dark bulk of a good-sized cabin built close to the gorge wall. Just beyond it a small stream ran across the canyon to vanish into the brush.

The cabin wall that faced Vane was cut by a door and a single window. The door was closed. The window was dark. No plume of smoke rose from the mud and stick chimney. Beyond the cabin he could make out a lean-to, apparently for the accommodation of horses. He could see that it was empty.

For minutes he sat staring at the cabin, until he was convinced it was untenanted. He sent Smoke forward, pulled him up before the closed door. There was still no sign or sound of life about the building. He swung to the ground and, hands close to his guns, advanced to the door. A moment later he swung it open with a strong shove, instantly stepping to one side as he did so.

Nothing happened. The cabin remained silent. Vane stepped through the opening.

There was still sufficient light to reveal the interior plainly. A swift, all-embracing glance showed the Ranger a roughly but comfortably furnished room with abunks built along the walls, peg-racks upon which hung rifles, bridles and saddles, a table, several chairs, a stove, and shelves stocked with staple provisions.

"This is it, all right!" he exulted.

He advanced to examine the rifles. His eyes glowed as he found that several of them were the odd .32-.20 calibre. On a lower shelf, boxes of cartridges were stacked. He squatted beside the shelf and pulled several out of place, noting the calibre.

"Now if I could just hit on a short gun that'll take these," he muttered, "it would—"

He twisted about as a shadow fell across his shoulder. In the doorway loomed the figure of a man. There was a flash of fire, the crash of a report, echoed by the thud of the Desert Rider's body striking the floor.

CHAPTER XVII

In his private car at the scene of the bore through the Chamizal Hills, Matthew Clemon, president of the M & K Railroad, sat at a table desk opening and closing his powerful hands in evident agitation. There was sweat on the railroad president's bad-tempered face. His eyes shifted constantly from side to side. He wet his dry lips with the tip of his tongue.

"I tell you, Hardin, you've gone too far!" he cried hoarsely at the man who sat across the desk.

Wesley Hardin, his handsome face undisturbed, an amused light in his keen eyes, regarded Clemon in silence. He raised his cigarette with a steady hand, let a trickle of smoke escape between his lips. The lips twisted slightly in a sneer.

"I told you I didn't want any killings," Clemon continued, his fingers tapping a nervous tattoo on the table top, "and now look what's happened."

Hardin spoke, his voice steady. "Hired me to slow

up the C & P, didn't you?" he remarked. "Well, I've slowed 'em, and slowed 'em good. That material train smash-up caused 'em to lose days of time, and bustin' down the facin' in the cut set 'em back a whole week. If that fire last night had acted like it was supposed to have, they'd be sunk."

"Yes, but two laborers lost their lives in the dynamite explosion in the cut," quavered Clemon. "I tell you it was murder, just like the killing of that brakeman and fireman. If it ever comes out Hardin, you'll hang."

The sarcastic smile left Hardin's firm lips. His eyes hardened. He leaned forward, fixed the other with his cold gaze.

"Listen, Matt," he said, "if I hang, I won't hang alone. You're in this just as deep as I am, and don't forget it."

More sweat appeared on Clemon's livid face. He glanced wildly about, as if seeking some way out from the predicament in which he found himself.

"When you start playin' this kind of a game, you head for trouble," Hardin continued. "Accidents are bound to happen. I didn't start out to kill anybody doin' those chores, but that's the way things worked out."

"I don't know what's come over you of late," complained the railroader. "You never used to handle things like that. You were always smart, but out here you don't seem to give a darn."

"Maybe I'm tired of workin' for wages," Hardin interposed quietly. "Maybe I'm out to grab off all I can, like you are. Ever consider than angle, Clemon?"

The other clenched his fists, opened them, clenched them again. "The sheriff was up here talking to me about that wreck," he said. "I tell you he's suspicious as anything."

"Old Hilton couldn't track a herd of buffalo across a snowed-over pasture," Hardin returned contemptuously.

"And that isn't all that's worrying me," Clemon continued, "if things aren't handled more carefully from now on, we'll have Rangers over here."

"Oh, don't let that worry you," Hardin replied calmly, "we've already got a Ranger here."

"What!"

"Uh-huh, remember that big feller you had the row with down on the grade the other day, the one who kept the dynamite cars from blowing Sanders to Mexico?"

Clemon's agitation was abruptly swallowed by black rage. "That cowhand!" he spat. "I wish I'd gone back with another gun and shot him, like I wanted to when you stopped me."

"Reckon it's a good thing you didn't try it," Hardin

replied dryly. "You would have been dead before you reached. I recognized him for what he is that first day in Sanders, and so did Cale Barnes. He was with Captain Burks over in the Nueces country when we were there. He's the chief reason we pulled out of the Nueces. Thank Pete he never saw us over there—I hope!"

"And you think he's a Ranger?" quavered Clemon.

"Oh, he's a Ranger, all right," Hardin replied. "And, Matt, ever hear of the Desert Rider?"

Clemon nearly leaped from his chair. "What!" he gasped.

"See you have," Hardin nodded. "Uh-huh, that's the Desert Rider, McNelty's ace man. Old Jim evidently sent him here to look things over. Now you see what we're up against."

Clemon sank back in his chair. His hands shook. His face was a dirty gray in color and now literally streamed sweat.

"What are we going to do?" he asked in a thick voice.

Hardin's lips writhed in a wolfish grin. His eyes seemed flickers of blue flame. He leaned forward.

"There's just one thing to do, and I'll do it," he said. "We made two tries for him that first day, but each time he slipped out of the noose. The next time he won't."

Clemon's face seemed to sink in, his eyes to glaze. "Kill a Ranger!" he whispered. "We'll have McNelty and his whole company over here!"

"McNelty won't learn what's happened until it's too late to do him any good," Hardin replied. "His Desert Rider will disappear, that's all."

A little later Hardin left the coach. He mounted his splendid bay horse and rode slowly west toward the hills, paralleling the tracks. He pulled up beside a clump of thicket close to where the cut in the hills began. A man stepped from the thicket and glanced up at him. It was Cale Barnes.

"Well?" he asked expectantly.

"Well," Hardin replied, "his nerve is plumb busted. I don't trust him any more."

The other looked concerned. Hardin leaned closer. "Cale," he said softly, "I've a notion the M & K needs a new president."

Hardin's range boss met his gaze, nodded in perfect understanding. "Uh-huh," he agreed, "I've a notion you're right. Not that I blame Clemon for feeling like he does," he added, his voice querulous. "I ain't feelin' so good myself, the way things have been going. That blasted Desert Rider! Sometimes I think he ain't human!"

"He's a man with the forked end down and a hat on top, just like the rest of us!" Hardin returned angrily.

"And with something besides hair and bone under the hat," Barnes grunted.

"Nothing a well placed slug won't take care of," said Hardin. "The devil with him for the time bein'! You got a chore to do, and see that you don't make some fool slip."

It was fully dark when Matthew Clemon's combination cook and porter pattered back from the little kitchen compartment in the front end of the private car to inform his boss that dinner was ready. He found the office compartment unlighted.

"Now where's de boss man got hisself to?" he grumbled, striking a match and touching it to the wick of a bracket lamp.

The soft glow revealed Clemon lolling back in his desk chair, his eyes half closed, his mouth open, his arm hanging limply by his side.

"Wake up, Boss," the darky began. "It's time to— Gawd A'mighty!"

Eyes bulging, jaw sagging, the Negro stared at the awful figure in the chair. Then with a howl of terror, he whirled and fled madly toward the outside.

Matthew Clemon remained lolling back in his chair, his white shirt front stained scarlet, a knife driven sideways through his throat.

CHAPTER XVIII

In the doorway of the cabin in the gorge, the owl-hoot, his gun muzzle wisping smoke, stood peering at the sprawled figure on the floor. Vane lay on his face, his head turned slightly sideways, his arms flung forward, the hands hanging limp. Beside his head, a dark smudge of blood stained the floor boards.

The owlhoot hesitated, still peering with outthrust neck. He took a step forward, then halted, gun ready. With a grunt of satisfaction he advanced on his victim, lowering his gun. He started to bend over the body. He yelled in terror as hands seized his ankles in a grip of steel. He fired wildly as his feet were jerked from under him and he hit the floor with a crash. Before he could pull trigger a second time, Vane's grip fixed on his wrist, bending his arm back and down. The gun exploded with a roar under the mechanical jerk of his finger. He gave a queer gasping grunt and the gun fell from his grasp. Then his heels beat a weird tattoo on the floor boards and were still.

Cautiously Vane eased his grip on the limp wrist. He stared down at the distorted face. Then he got to his feet and fingered the bullet graze just above his own left temple.

"Drilled himself dead center," he muttered, gazing down at the dead man. "Well, that one was touch-and-go. If I hadn't fooled him when I pitched myself over, he'd have plugged me full of holes before I could draw. Came nigh on to doing a finish job as it was. An inch to the right and it would have been curtains. Well, I asked for it. Of all the loco tricks! Leaving Smoke standing outside the shack in plain sight! Now I've got to get away from here before some more visitors show up. That would be a mite too interesting, to say nothing of scrambling all my plans for fair."

Picking up the body, he carried it outside and dropped it to the ground. He hurried back into the cabin, found a rag and removed the blood stains from the boards as best he could. He scuffed dust over the spots with his boots.

"Have to do," he muttered. "Chances are they won't be noticed."

He hurried out again, closing the door behind him.

The owlhoot's horse stood a little distance up the trail, reins hanging. He caught the animal and draped the body over the saddle. With the outlaw's rope he tied the body securely. Suddenly he lifted his head. From the bend in the canyon sounded a faint clicking. Seizing the horses' reins, he hurried down canyon with them, slid into the brush, moved forward a little farther and halted.

"Now don't one of you jugheads get a notion to sing a song to the stars," he breathed. He stood ready to grab a nose at the first indication of a neigh.

A pounding of hoofs sounded from the direction of the cabin, ceased abruptly. Vane heard a murmur of voices. A little later the cabin door banged. He waited a moment or two, then moved forward cautiously, pausing frequently to listen.

But the darkening canyon remained silent. He mounted Smoke and, leading the burdened horse, rode down-canyon through the thickening gloom.

Overhead the stars had vanished under a thick blanket of cloud, on the sable bosom of which lightning flickered. A rumble of thunder shook the air. A breath of wind fanned Vane's face, died to nothingness. It returned as a gust, increased in power. A drop of icy rain stung Vane's face. Others followed. Then with a roar and a bellow the storm burst in full force.

Beaten, blinded, drenched to the skin, Vane bowed

his head to the lash of the rain and rode on. The horses snorted and shivered in abject fear. Vane shouted encouragement to them, his voice drowned by the bellow of the thunder and the howling of the wind. With a terrific crash a section of cliff rushed down under the stroke of a lightning bolt. The accompanying peal of thunder was deafening. As it died away, Vane was conscious of a deep-toned roaring somewhere ahead. It increased in volume, shaking the air with its awesome diapason.

Suddenly Smoke halted, snorting and shivering. The lead horse neighed thinly and pulled back. The lightning blazed from horizon to zenith, and in its frightful glare Vane saw such a sight as he hoped never to see again.

Under his very elbow was a sheer drop into the depths of a canyon. The canyon was half filled with raging, tossing black water flecked with bits of foam. The lightning blazed again, revealing, a thousand feet or so across the gorge, a torrent of water hurtling downward from a cliff top. The yellow glare turned it to a cataract of flame ringed about by a spray of multi-colored fires. The canyon was a caldron of molten brass spangled and flecked with ruddy gold, a yawning mouth threatening to engulf the earth.

Cautiously Vane reined Smoke around and headed him away from the pit of terrors. The rain beat against his face. He was pounded by spouts of water hurtling down from the cliffs, blinded by the lightning and the moments of stygian blackness that followed. He felt his senses were going; his body was numb with cold, his teeth chattering. Every moment the tearing wind threatened to hurl him from the saddle to destruction.

And then abruptly the force of the wind lessened somewhat, the rain beat with less violence. A flare of lightning revealed that he was riding along the face of an overhanging cliff. He crowded Smoke against the rock, thankful for even the uncertain shelter of the overhang. A lightning flash revealed a dark cleft or opening in the rock a few feet ahead, from which ghostly hands seemed to beckon.

"Into there, feller," he gasped, turning the moros' head. Wet leaves and twigs slapped his face and hands. There was a crackling and breaking sound. Another moment and Smoke's irons rang hollow echoes. The wind ceased suddenly. The rain no longer beat upon them.

Vane halted the horses. In a pocket he had matches in a corked bottle. He managed to get one out without wetting the head. He slid his rifle from the boot, opened the lock and scratched the match on the dry metal. It flared up with a tiny flame, revealing rock walls on either side and a rocky ceiling just above his head.

"A cave!" the Ranger muttered thankfully. He sent Smoke forward a few more paces, halted him and dismounted, stiff and sore in every muscle. His boots crunched on something that gave beneath them. He managed to get another match going. The glow showed the cave floor littered with dry leaves and tendrils fallen in the course of the years from a mass of vines hanging down the cliff face, and heaped inside the cave by the wind. He raked an armload together and touched a match to the mound. It caught fire quickly and burned with a bright flame. Vane gathered more twigs and built up the fire. Soon he had a roaring blaze going, which he fed with stout sections of vine lying nearer the entrance of the cave. When the fire was going to his satisfaction, he removed the body of the owlhoot from the horse's back and laid it alongside the wall. Then he got the wet rigs off both horses and rubbed them down as well as he was able. He heaped more fuel on the fire, poured the water from his boots, wrung out his sodden garments as much as he could and stood steaming before the blaze.

The fierce heat quickly dried his clothes and beat the chill from his bones. He built up the fire still more, curled up beside it and went to sleep.

The fire had burned to a gray ash when Vane awakened, but the air was warm and sunlight was pouring a flood of green and gold through the vines that hung down the cliff. Smoke and the outlaw's horse had moved to the front of the cave and were munching mouthfuls of green leaves.

Vane struggled into his water-stiffened boots and walked to the mouth of the cave. He found he was on the eastern slope of the Chamizals. Below lay the rangeland, a sea of emerald in the sunlight. He estimated that the Cross C ranchhouse should be almost due east from where he stood, and perhaps a dozen miles distant. The slopes were steep but the descent did not appear impossible. He returned to the cave and dragged the body of the outlaw to the light. He proved to be a hard-looking individual without anything outstanding about him. His pockets revealed nothing of significance.

"Reckon I'll just leave you here, feller," he told the dead man. "Can't very well pack you in without attracting attention. I'll let your pals do some wondering as to what became of you. That's okay by me, so long as they don't guess the truth, and I don't figure they will."

He got the rig on Smoke, bridled the outlaw's horse but left its saddle lying where it was. At the base of the slope he removed the animal's bridle, and turned him loose to graze. Then he rode swiftly across the prairie, speedily got his bearings and headed for the ranchhouse, which he reached well before noon.

"Got caught in the storm, eh?" old Clate remarked as he rode into the yard.

"That's right," Vane said. "Holed up for the night under a cliff."

Bradshaw nodded, such occurrences not being unusual on the rangeland.

"Get into some fresh clothes and come on and eat," he said. "Reckon you could stand a s'roundin'."

They had just finished their meal when Sheriff Hilton and the coroner rode up to the ranchhouse.

"Where you headed for?" Bradshaw asked.

"Up to the M & K camp," Hilton replied. "Matthew Clemon, the M & K president, got hisself murdered up there last night."

"What!" exclaimed Bradshaw. Vane regarded the sheriff with narrowed eyes.

"Uh-huh," Hilton nodded. "Somebody stuck a knife through his neck, accordin' to the word I got this mornin'. I ain't surprised, though. He was pretty well hated by the folks who worked under him. Reckon he went a mite too far with somebody."

"Don't know who did it, then?"

"Nope. His cook found him when he went to call

him to dinner, or so I was told. He'd been seen out on the grade about an hour before. Went back to his coach just before dark, and that was the last time anybody saw him alive, except the jigger who did for him, of course. There sure 'pears to be a cuss on this section of late."

After a cup of coffee, the sheriff and coroner rode on. Old Clate shook his grizzled head as he watched them depart.

"Poor old Boone sure has got his troubles," he remarked of the sheriff. "Just one darn thing after another."

Vane rode to Sanders the following morning and at once repaired to the telegraph office. There he found a long message from Captain McNelty:

YOUR MAN HARDIN SEEMS OKAY. I WIRED HUGHES ON RECEIPT OF YOUR MESSAGE. HUGHES GOT ON THE JOB. AND HUGHES IS THOROUGH. HARDIN IS FAIRLY WELL KNOWN IN THE NUECES COUNTRY AND IN SAN ANTONIO. REPUTATION FOR BEING SALTY AND SMART. NOTHING AGAINST HIM THAT HUGHES COULD LEARN. ORIGINS VAGUE. BANK REFERENCES AUTHENTIC. BEEN CONNECTED WITH M & K RAILROAD FOR SEVERAL YEARS. SORT OF TROUBLE SHOOTER FOR PRESIDENT MATTHEW CLEMON. HELPED CLEMON WITH SOME OF HIS QUESTIONABLE DEALS. CLEMON ALWAYS KEEPS INSIDE LAW SO FAR AS IS KNOWN. HARDIN LEFT THE NUECES COUNTRY ABOUT

A YEAR BACK WITH A HERD OF COWS HE BOUGHT.
DROPPED OUT OF SIGHT.

Vane read the terse sentences several times. Then he folded the sheet and carefully stowed it away. For some moments he stood gazing into the distance.

So that's why Ron Sealy was killed! he mused.

CHAPTER XIX

Vane shrugged his broad shoulders and headed for the sheriff's office. He found Sheriff Hilton at his desk. The lines in the old peace officer's face seemed deeper, the worried look about his eyes intensified.

"Now what?" he asked as Vane entered. "Trouble up to the Cross C, I suppose. Well, it's to be expected. Trouble's all I hear about of late."

Vane smiled and shook his head. He drew a chair to the desk and sat down. He was fumbling with a cunningly concealed secret pocket in his broad leather belt. He laid something on the desk between them.

Sheriff Hilton stared at the glittering object, his eyes widening. It was a gleaming silver star set on a silver circle, the honored badge of the Texas Rangers!

For a moment the sheriff seemed bereft of speech. Then he raised his eyes to Vane's face. "A Ranger!" he sputtered. "So you're a Texas Ranger!" Abruptly he leaped to his feet, his face wild with excitement.

"Son!" he exclaimed, "I've got you placed. I had a feelin' your name was familiar the first time I heard it, but Vane is a fairly common name in the Southwest and I didn't pay it much mind. But now I know. Tom Vane! Son, you're the Desert Rider!"

"Been called that," Vane admitted smilingly.

Sheriff Hilton stared, almost in awe, at the legendary figure whose exploits were the talk of the Southwest. "The Desert Rider!" he repeated. "Well, I'd ought to have knowed it. You been doin' the kind of things since you landed in this section that folks say the Desert Rider is always doin'. So McNelty sent you here, eh?"

"That's right," Vane replied. "He figured you could use a little help."

Sheriff Hilton had the look of a man who had abruptly been relieved of a burden too heavy for his strength.

"What's in line? What have you found out?" he asked.

Vane told him. The sheriff swore in amazement as the case unfolded.

"Wes Hardin!" he exclaimed. "I never would have believed it. There never seemed to be a squarer feller. Well, if this don't take the shingles off the barn! What do you want me to do? Ride up and corral the sidewinder?"

Vane shook his head. "We have absolutely no case against him yet," he replied. "Yes, I know, I saw him forking that Hearn & Bledsoe saddle the day he rode up to the private car to visit with Clemon. That's what gave me my first real line on him. But he wouldn't have the least trouble explaining that. He could say he bought it from somebody or that the jigger who bought it from Calloway was in his employ at the time and left it shortly afterwards. Nothing against him there. Yes, as you say, you learned he visited Clemon the afternoon of the day Clemon was killed. But you admit you also learned that Clemon was seen out on the grade *after* Hardin rode away from the car. I learned that Hardin was in the employ of the M & K over in the Nueces country. What of it? He left the Nueces country about a year ago with a herd of cows. He had quit the railroad and was going into the cattle business. No reason why he should tell folks out here he once worked for the railroad, especially as nobody ever asked him. Perfectly natural he should visit Clemon, the man he once worked for. I'm positive he killed Ron Sealy, but I have no proof. Why did he kill Sealy? Because Sealy, making a routine check on his bank references when Hardin wanted to buy a herd from Bradshaw, on time, wrote to his brother in San Antonio who is a banker. The brother wrote him the whole low-down on Hardin. I gather that Sealy never did like Hardin over well and aimed to tell Bradshaw about his railroad connections, knowing that Bradshaw would go up in the air, having no use for the railroads. That's why Sealy was having so much fun with Bradshaw when Bradshaw was cussing Wade Fulton and standing up for Hardin. Right there Sealy signed his own death warrant. Sealy didn't realize how important the matter was to Hardin."

"Why was it so important to him?"

"Because," Vane replied slowly, "Hardin had his eye on the Cross C spread. He'd managed to get in with Bradshaw and cause Clate to think well of him. He figured to marry Bradshaw's daughter, that's all."

"The hyderphobia skunk!" the sheriff growled.

"Hardin either caught on to what Sealy knew, or Sealy told him that morning when they were riding to town together, or perhaps before," Vane continued. "Yes, I'm pretty sure Hardin caught up with Sealy that morning. Might have been keeping an eye on him all the time waiting for a chance. Sealy, of course, had no reason to suspect Hardin had designs on his life. Hardin shot him in the back of the head as they were riding along. Then he cut across the prairie and hightailed to town. You'll remember, he got in town just a little while before I did the morning Sealy was killed. He aims to get Wade Fulton out of the way, also, and I wouldn't be a mite surprised if I'm down in his brand blotting book, too. In fact, I'm pretty sure he has already made a couple of tries for me. First when the drygulching was staged in the Devil's Kitchen while we were trailing them after the fireman and brakeman of the dynamite train were killed. Again that night in the Greasy Sack when the row broke between the Cross C boys and the C & P railroaders. Hardin arranged that rukus, playing on Bull Masters' habit of flying off the handle at the least provocation. If things had really got going good, I've a notion I might have stopped a convenient stray slug. Regrettable 'accident,' of course. He'll make another try the first chance he gets."

"And what in blazes are we goin' to do about it?" the sheriff demanded helplessly.

"Wait," Vane replied. "That's all we can do. Wait, and keep our eyes skun. Sooner or later he and his bunch are going to bust loose again. Then we'll swoop down on their hole-up and bag the lot of them."

Sheriff Hilton tugged his mustache reflectively. "Somethin' might bust loose right here in town tomorrow," he observed. "Tomorrow is payday for the C & P. They're paying off here now instead of at Sanders. Roma's nearer railhead and they can get their workers back easier after their payday bust. Everybody will be in town spendin' money like water.

'Most anything could happen. I'm on the lookout for trouble. There'll be plenty of dinero in various saloon safes by tomorrow night. A bunch like that might make a try for some of it."

"You may have something there," Vane agreed thoughtfully. "Okay, I'll ride in again late tonight and be with you tomorrow. Got plenty of special deputies sworn in?"

Roma wore a festive air the following morning. Shop and saloon doors stood wide open. Already the board sidewalks were packed with a cheerful, jostling throng.

The greatest crowd, however, had gathered around the railroad station. All eyes were turned to the east, for from the east would come the paycar bearing the many thousands of dollars that would be shoved through the grated windows into the eager hands of the workers.

Some three miles to the east the railroad vanished into a cut that bored through the low hills that slashed the skyline. On the south side of the tracks the rangeland shimmered, gradually merging with the desert to the south, but on the north the hills sent out a long spur that ended less than a mile from town. This broad spur extended into the north for many miles in a series of rolling rises cut by shallow canyons and wide draws grown thickly with grass and weeds. The south slopes of the spur ran to within a few hundred yards of the tracks before petering out in the monotonous level of the flats.

Over to one side, near the spur onto which the paycar would be shunted, stood Sheriff Hilton and Tom Vane watching the crowd.

From the roof of the station suddenly sounded an exultant whoop. A man there was dancing precariously on the sloping shingles, yelling and waving his arms.

"Pa-a-ay dirt!" he howled. "Here she comes, boys!"

The crowd seethed and jostled with excitement, straining their eyes toward the sun-drenched east. At first they could see nothing but a wavering plume of dark smoke advancing swiftly toward the town. Then under the smoke cloud appeared a crawling dot that quickly gained size and shape. The crowd cheered wildly and tossed hats into the air. A moment later a mellow whistle note sounded, thin with distance. Another cheer shook the air.

On came the paycar, exhaust pounding, smoke boiling from the locomotive's stack. It was less than two miles from the town now, and drawing nearer with every turn of the spinning wheels.

And then abruptly a cloud of yellowish smoke gushed into the air directly in front of the pilot of the speeding engine. The train vanished into the spreading pall. An instant later the dull boom of an explosion reached the ears of the crowd. From the dark slopes to the north ran a number of figures. The crowd could see the puffs of whitish smoke as guns blazed. The yellowish pall thinned and revealed the paycar engine lying on its side and spouting steam. The car itself was jammed against the overturned locomotive. For an instant it stood out hard and clear in the sunlight; then it was enveloped in another cloud of smoke. The crash of another explosion quivered the air.

From the crowd rose a wild roar of rage. "A hold-up!" howled a voice. "They've wrecked the paycar! They're stealin' our money!"

Bellowing, raving, howling curses, the crowd streamed eastward across the range.

CHAPTER XX

The instant the first explosion sounded the sheriff bounded forward, cursing. But Vane gripped his arm.

"Hold it," he cautioned. "There's nothing you can do now. It's two miles away, and you could never get there in time. And even if you could, you couldn't face rifle fire across those flats. They'd down every one of us. Wait and see what happens. They put it over on us, that's all, but this may be the break we need."

Again the smoke thinned. Men could be seen standing around the paycar. In a moment others came out the door, bearing burdens.

"The hellions are cleanin' up!" rasped the sheriff, fairly dancing with anger and excitement. "The paymaster would have the safe open now, and all they have to do is scoop up the dinero and hightail."

"Smart, all right," Vane agreed. "Waited till they were in sight of town and the safes would be open.

I'm afraid it's too bad for some of those poor devils in the car. There the hellions go, heading for the hills. They'll have horses waiting. All right, now. Get your posse together. We'll want a dozen men. Tell them to put some chuck in their saddle pouches. They'll need it."

The deputies were already crowding around, shaking their fists and swearing. "Get your bronks," the sheriff told them, "and get all set for hard riding." He passed on Vane's orders, which were swiftly obeyed. Ten minutes after the first explosion the posse thundered out of town, Vane and the sheriff riding in front.

They passed the straggling throng of railroad workers and surged up to the paycar. It was badly wrecked by the dynamite explosions. The fireman and engineer had almost miraculously escaped with minor injuries, but one of the guards was dead, another badly wounded. The paymaster had a gashed head and one of his clerks had suffered a broken arm.

"They got everything," the paymaster told Sheriff Hilton. "We tried to put up a fight but we never had a chance. The first explosion and the wreck just about knocked us out. Then they threw a stick of powder through the window. That's what killed the guard. The rest of us were stunned, and before we got our senses back they were all over us. Yes, they were masked. Seemed to be about a dozen of 'em. May have been more back in the brush."

The construction workers were streaming up to the car. "Look after the fellows who are hurt," Vane told them. "All right, Sheriff, let's go."

They rode into the brush that clothed the slope, and quickly discovered where the outlaws had tethered their horses. After scouting about a little, Vane picked up the trail, which led northeast. The posse set out to follow it at a fast clip. But once they were well into the hills, Vane slowed the pace.

"We'll likely need all our horses can do before we're finished," he told Hilton. "I'm playing my hunch, and if it proves straight, the thieves will get the surprise of their lives tonight."

"Figger they're headed for the east hills?" Hilton asked.

Vane nodded. "That's where they'll figure us to lose the trail. They've got a good start, and they'll keep ambling around till it gets dark. Then they'll cut loose and head west to their hangout, or I'm a heap mistaken. They know we can't catch up with them, and once it gets dark, it will be easy to shake us. They'll work on the notion that we'll figure they'll keep on heading east through the hills, which is the logical thing for them to do. Okay, let them do the figuring. We know just what we're going to do."

Until well past noon, Vane led the posse through the hills at a leisurely pace. In a leafy hollow he called a halt.

"We'll eat our chuck and rest the horses," he told the possemen. "Nothing to do for a while but take it easy."

Men were posted amid the brush on the lip of the hollow to guard against possible spying, but as the afternoon wore on they reported no sign of the owlhoots. The sun was low in the west when Vane ordered his men to mount again. He rode at their head, his face bleak, his eyes coldly gray. On his broad breast gleamed the star of the Rangers. Behind him, the possemen stared and whispered. Sheriff Hilton had revealed Vane's identity and had created plenty of excitement.

The sun sank behind the Chamizals, the shadows deepened. It was dark when they rode down the slope of the hills and out onto the rangeland. Here Vane quickened the pace and they went almost due west. They reached Big Bowl Canyon, threaded the narrow gorge and crossed the wide amphitheatre to the west. Cautiously they made their way up the steep western slope, across the valley on the far side and into the hidden canyon. Overhead the stars spangled the sky with silver. The night was very still, but with a faint breeze blowing from the west.

Where the canyon began to veer to the south, Vane halted the posse.

"We'll leave the horses here and go ahead on foot," he told his men. "The click of irons would carry a long way in this silence."

With the greatest care the posse stole forward. "I smell smoke," the sheriff whispered.

"They're here, all right," Vane returned, "and I'm counting on the whole pack. The big he-wolf is with them, I figure. There's a lot of dinero to be divided, and he'd hardly leave that to anyone else. That breed doesn't trust one another over well."

"How you figger to work it?" the sheriff asked.

"We'll get as close to the cabin as we can, then rush 'em," Vane replied. "We'll hardly get by without a shooting. Let 'em have it as soon as we're inside. Everything should be to our advantage, but we can't afford to take chances with this bunch."

Carefully and slowly they wormed their way through the growth, pausing often to peer and listen, advancing a few paces, then halting to stand rigid with straining ears. After what seemed a very long time they reached the final fringe of growth and peered cautiously ahead. The cabin loomed dark and shadowy. Light streamed through the window. The door was closed. And in front of the door, walking slowly up and down at the edge of the growth, was a man.

"Now what?" breathed the sheriff in Vane's ear. "If that hellion spots us and lets out a yelp, it'll be mighty bad."

Vane held up his hand for quiet. In utter silence he slid into the growth and vanished from sight.

Rigid, sweating, their nerves crawling with apprehension, the possemen crouched in the brush and waited, their eyes fixed on the slowly strolling figure of the guard. They saw him pass close to the edge of the growth, turn and stroll back. They could see his eye glint as they swept the brush at the bend of the trail, where they crouched waiting. Then he turned once more and sauntered away from them.

Behind the guard a tall figure materialized from the thicket. The posse saw Vane steal forward on the guard's track, make a panther-like bound. Vane's arm rose and fell. The guard pitched forward on his face and lay sprawled and motionless. Vane turned and glided into the shadow of the brush.

"Bent a gun barrel over his head," Sheriff Hilton muttered. "Well, that takes care of that."

A moment later, Vane loomed beside the sheriff. "Okay," he breathed, "let's go. Quiet, but fast. We've got to get the jump on them."

The posse moved forward swiftly, crossed the little open space, reached the cabin. Vane hit the door with his shoulder, slamming it back against the wall, and leaped into the room, the posse bulging after him. His voice rang out:

"In the name of the State of Texas! Throw up your hands!"

Seated at the table were nearly a dozen men, Wesley Hardin at the far end, facing the door. The table was littered with stacks of gold pieces.

For a crawling instant the owlhoots sat stunned. Then, with a yell of fear and fury, Wes Hardin leaped to his feet, his hand streaking to his armpit.

But even as his gun flashed into sight, Vane shot him. Hardin reeled back, blood gushing from his mouth, his eyes wild and staring. But so great was his vitality, he managed to swing the gun around and fire one shot before he fell, his chest smashed and riddled by the Ranger's bullets. The cabin rocked and shivered to the roar of gunfire.

Caught settin', utterly unprepared for the attack, the owlhoots never had a chance. In a matter of seconds, half of their number were down. The others dropped their guns, cringed behind tables and chairs and howled for mercy.

As Sheriff Hilton and the possemen began securing the prisoners, Vane strode forward among the fallen.

He picked up a gun from beside the dead Wesley Hardin and handed it to the sheriff.

"Here's the .32-.20 that killed Ron Sealy," he remarked.

Among the badly wounded was Cale Barnes, Hardin's range boss. The fear of imminent death had shaken Barnes' soul and he readily gasped out answers to Vane's questions.

"I just about figured the thing right," Vane told Sheriff Hilton as they rode to town with the prisoners and the recovered payroll gold. "Matthew Clemon, a smart railroader, realized that the real fight between the M & K and the C & P in their road-building race would begin when they started the bore through the Chamizal Hills. So last year he sent Hardin over, posing as a cattleman, to get placed and delay the C & P all he could. Hardin did a good chore at delaying the C & P all right, but he got completely out of hand. When he landed in this section he saw there were fine pickings to be had. So he called in his bunch from the Nueces country and proceeded to feather his own nest proper. Clemon knew what was going on but couldn't stop it. Finally he got badly scared. Hardin and Barnes were afraid he'd double-cross them in an effort to save his own neck, so Barnes, acting on Hardin's orders, killed Clemon. They had already spotted me as a Ranger, and I reckon Hardin was getting sort of jumpy himself, especially as things were beginning to break wrong for him."

"Like losing out on his try at rustling the herd Bradshaw sold to George Godfrey," suggested the sheriff.

Vane nodded and paused to roll a cigarette. "Yes, things began to break wrong for him there. He made a bad mistake when he forgot to get that saddle receipt from his hand who bought the saddle for him. Of course, his bad break was when that jigger went and got himself killed and I found the receipt in his pocket. Hardin also made a mistake when he dickered to buy the herd from Bradshaw, although he had no way of knowing that he was doing so. If Ron Sealy hadn't had a brother in San Antonio who was a banker, he would have just written to Hardin's San Antonio bank and gotten a reply that Hardin's bank references were okay. But Sealy's brother dug up everything he could on Hardin that he thought might be of interest to Ron. Hardin slipped a mite again when he tried to plant his range boss, Barnes, with Bradshaw. He figured he was playing smart there, but it set me to thinking harder about him. The thing looked a little funny to me. His liking for .32-.20 calibre guns didn't help him, either."

"How's that?" asked the sheriff.

"Well," Vane replied, "that's a calibre seldom seen in the Southwest, although I've run across quite a few of them further east. It's a gun that is liked in the river bottoms over there where folks use 'em in hunting bear and deer in the thick growth. They pack a good wallop and they're short rifles, easy to handle in dense bush. It set me thinking about somebody from over east who might have brought one here with him. Well, Hardin was from over east. A little thing, but enough little threads wound together make a strong cord, and I was already tying up a lot of loose threads."

"Yes," the sheriff nodded thoughtfully, "just a lot of little loose threads that didn't mean a thing to most folks, but they meant plenty to the Desert Rider. Well, I reckon that's why he's the Desert Rider!"

Two days later Tom Vane reined in his blue horse where the notch trail flowed across the lofty crest of the Chamizal Hills. His sternly handsome face showed a quiet contentment as he gazed back at the emerald billows of the rangeland far below. He had ridden into a section torn by strife, hatred, prejudice and lawlessness. Behind him he was leaving peace and order and happiness and good fellowship. With a smile in his eyes he rode on into the pass to where duty called and new adventure waited.